For Granny and Jacob – oldest and newest members of the family!

A.P.

This is a work of fiction. Names, characters, places and incidents are either the product of the author's imagination or, if real, used fictitiously. All statements, activities, stunts, descriptions, information and material of any other kind contained herein are included for entertainment purposes only and should not be relied on for accuracy or replicated as they may result in injury.

First published 2026 by Walker Books Ltd
87 Vauxhall Walk, London SE11 5HJ

2 4 6 8 10 9 7 5 3 1

EU Authorized Representative: HackettFlynn Ltd
36 Cloch Choirneal, Balrothery, Co. Dublin, K32 C942, Ireland
EU@walkerpublishinggroup.com

This book has been typeset in Source Serif Pro and Dekko

Printed and bound by CPI Group (UK) Ltd, Croydon CR0 4YY

British Library Cataloguing in Publication Data:
a catalogue record for this book is available from the British Library

ISBN 978-1-5295-1971-6

www.walker.co.uk

FSC www.fsc.org MIX Paper | Supporting responsible forestry FSC® C013604

WALKER BOOKS

ALICE PRIMMER

ILLUSTRATED BY FRED BLUNT

THE WORLD'S WORST ALIEN

FIGHTS BACK

Imagine a perfect world.

Imagine a world without war.

Imagine a world without pollution.

Imagine a world where your little brother never annoys you, where it never rains if you forgot your umbrella, where every crisp packet contains more crisps than you were expecting.

Imagine a world where the sky is made of rainbows, where unicorns dance in waterfalls, where the houses are built with ice cream.

Now imagine Earth. Does it have any of those things? No. Unfortunately, this is kind of my fault.

You see, when our teacher set my class an assignment to create a planet, my classmates stuffed theirs full of unicorns and rainbows and

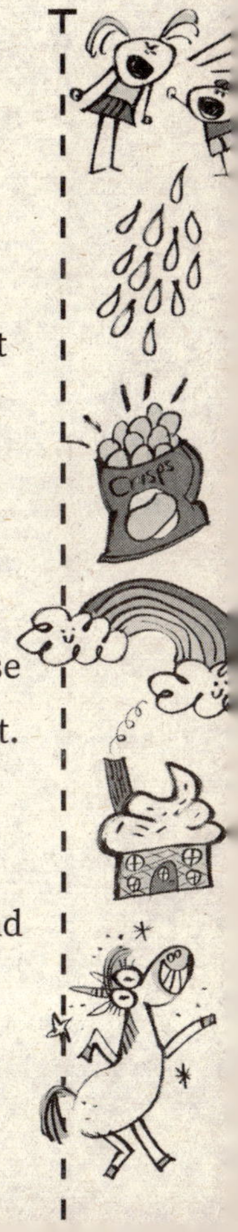

peace. I, on the other hand, forgot about my project until the last minute, when I discovered that my planet had been overrun with annoying creatures called humans.

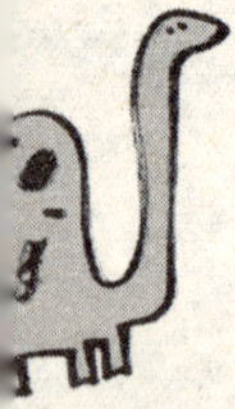

In my defence, I did try to fix it. I tried going down to Earth and getting rid of all those pesky humans and replacing them with something much better: dinosaurs. As it's you reading this, and not a triceratops, you can probably tell that didn't work.

But none of that mattered. Because the project was over.

Or at least, that's what I thought.

It turns out that you can only get so many bad grades before "I'll do better next time" stops sounding believable. Apparently, it was time to teach me a lesson, and not the sort of lesson that you can doze through and then leave when the bell goes. No, this lesson was about cleaning up your own mess. And that meant fixing the problems with planet Earth.

So, while my classmates moved on to more exciting projects, like black-hole surfing and

time travel, I was held back, trying to think of a way to solve Earth problems like war, climate change and half-empty crisp packets.

It was a big challenge for anyone to have to take on. It was even more of a challenge for someone as lazy as me to take on. But while I might not have managed to wipe out humans on my last visit to Earth, it wasn't a complete waste of time. I had done one good thing: I'd made a friend.

Friends are useful when you have a problem to solve. They can do a lot of the hard work for you. And if I was ever going to finish this project and finally learn how to surf a black hole, I was going to need all the help I could get.

I made my decision. I configured my physical manifestation calibrator. I set the coordinates on my trans-dimensional transporter. And I did what I'd hoped never to have to do again.

I went to Earth.

2

There were a lot of questions I should have asked myself before returning to Earth. What was I going to do once I got there? Was transforming myself into an eleven-year-old girl the best way to solve these big problems? And was there really no way I could bring back the dinosaurs?

If I'd actually thought to ask myself any of these questions, it might have concerned me that I didn't have the answers.

All I knew was that I was going straight back to the spot where I had left Earth the first time: Zana Jackson's bedroom.

Zana was my friend. She had looked after me when everyone else on the planet thought I was weird. (Zana probably thought I was weird too, but she was nice enough not to say it out loud.) She was helpful, determined and (mostly) very patient.

The only problem was, she was also asleep.

Zana's bedroom was almost completely dark, with only a soft glow coming from the lizard tank under her bed. I had forgotten that humans waste huge amounts of time lying with their eyes closed and snoring.

I crouched down to give my regards to Turing the lizard. He eyed me nervously, which wasn't surprising. Zana used to have two lizards. She still does, technically. It's just that one of them is now floating in another dimension, after it accidentally licked my trans-dimensional transporter. I had decided not to tell Zana this. She was sure to overreact and blame me.

I stood up again. Zana was still asleep. This was getting ridiculous. I had a planet to save.

Very, very gently, I prodded the snoring shape on the bed.

Nothing happened.

Very, very firmly, I prodded the snoring shape on the bed again.

A blue-haired head turned to face me.

"Whuh–**AAAARRGGHHH!**"

"Hello, Zana, it's me–"

The bedroom door burst open and the light switched on.

"Darling, what's—

AAAARRGGHHHH!"

Zana's mum staggered backwards, colliding with Zana's dad as he appeared in the doorway.

"Polly, what's—

AAAARRGGHHHH!"

Zana's parents tumbled to the floor of the corridor.

I sighed. "Has anyone got anything to say other than AAAARRGGHHH?"

Zana was rubbing her eyes. "Sky?"

"Yes, obviously," I replied. I'd accepted being called this slightly silly human name while I was on Earth, seeing as it required a minimum of seven tongues to be able to pronounce my real alien one.

Zana's mum peered round the bedroom door. "How did you get in?"

I hesitated. "It's probably best you don't know."

Zana's dad peered round Zana's mum. "Excuse me, but if you don't mind, I think perhaps you might like to consider, maybe leaving."

"It's the middle of the night," Zana noted, pointlessly, since I had worked that out several minutes ago. "Sky can't leave."

"She's broken in, Susan!" Zana's mum exclaimed. (There wasn't an extra person in the room called Susan, by the way – Zana's mum just didn't like Zana's nickname.) "You can't invite an intruder to stay for breakfast."

"Sky isn't an intruder, she's just lost."

"Lost?! I thought she lived in Antarctica? How could she possibly be *that* lost?" Zana's mum shrieked.

I decided it was best not to say anything in response, especially as no one had ever told me where Antarctica actually was. It would look too suspicious to ask now.

"We can sort this out in the morning. I'll get out the camp bed. Don't worry," Zana said.

Telling Zana's mum not to worry was like telling a giraffe to keep its head down, but it seemed to work anyway. Zana's parents reluctantly retreated, leaving me and Zana alone.

I remembered what I'd learnt about human greetings on my last visit, and waved.

Zana squinted at me. "Sky. I have a lot of questions. But I'm very tired and I have school in the morning. So I'm going to ask you them now and then let you get your answers ready while I sleep. OK?"

"Do I answer that now or later?"

I couldn't tell if Zana was fighting not to roll her eyes, or falling asleep. Eventually she sighed, and said, "Right: why are you back? Why did you arrive in the middle of the night? Are you going to try to wipe out humans again? Did you get a good grade for your project? And do you know where my lizard Berners-Lee went?" She checked her alarm clock. "You have exactly four hours."

She pulled her duvet over her head, then added in a muffled voice, "Please switch the light off."

I did as I was told. Zana had forgotten to get the camp bed out (which was fine, as I didn't need sleep anyway), so I sat down in the dark next to the lizard tank. The only question that really needed answering was whether Zana would help me with my project again. But Zana hadn't asked that, so I would have to instead. When Zana finally turned off her alarm the next morning, I was standing at her bedside, ready.

"I don't have the answers to all your questions," I said, as she yawned. "Which is partly because I forgot what they were and I didn't want to wake you up again to ask you. All you need to know is that I failed."

"What? Even after everything we did?"

"Yes," I sighed. "My teacher said Earth still has a lot of problems, and that I need to fix them. So here I am."

"What kind of problems?"

"War, climate change, corruption, crisp packets..." I listed.

"You need to fix all that, and you came back as an eleven-year-old girl," Zana said. Her eyebrows had shot up so high they were disappearing into her hair.

"Yes," I said. "Will you help?"

Zana flopped back onto her pillow. I hoped she wasn't going back to sleep already.

Eventually, she said, "Of course I'll help you, Sky. You're my friend, and I'm pleased to see you. It's just, all those problems. They're a bit ... big."

"Really?" I said. "Even the crisp packets?"

"I'm sure that wasn't exactly the kind of problem your teacher wanted you to sort out."

"OK, fine. Let's start with the first one," I said. "War. Fighting. Humans are always doing it. It's stupid. Let's stop it."

"Sky, you know I believe that we can do a lot to change the world for the better. But are you sure you wouldn't be better off coming back as an adult? Like a campaigner, or an activist?"

"If I hadn't come back as me, I wouldn't have been able to see you."

Zana smiled.

"And you wouldn't have been able to solve my problems for me," I added.

Zana frowned.

"OK. We're going to have to think about this a bit more. But right now, I have to go to school. And so do you."

"I am NOT going back to school!"

I cried, loud enough to make Turing cower in his tank.

"Where else are you going to go?" Zana pointed out, as she climbed out of bed. "My parents are going to have you out the door the second you've finished your cornflakes. So you might as well come with me."

Annoyingly, Zana was right. And I didn't even want any cornflakes.

3

As I sat on the bus in my scratchy borrowed uniform and we trundled towards Oak Lane Primary School, Zana did what she did best: talking.

"You've only been gone a few weeks, Sky, but you've missed loads. I've got so much to tell you! Everything has been *amazing*. It's so great being in Eco Club. Saira let me come over to her house during the holidays so we could make new recycling bins for the school.

"Unfortunately we made them out of cardboard, so the caretaker recycled them, but still – it was *amazing*. And Mr Martins let us do a sponsored silence in his lessons to raise money so we could fund a gorilla sanctuary in Uganda, and I'm going to volunteer there when I'm older, which will be *amazing*. And so many people are using the school hall now that it isn't a health and safety risk. So basically, if I had to describe how things have been, I would say..."

"Amazing?" I suggested.

"Exactly." Zana's eyes were very wide. "Absolutely no problems." She blinked very fast. "Nothing is wrong." She shook her head so hard her face went blurry. "So don't even ask."

"OK, great, I won't. Now, back to me and *my* problems," I said, settling back in my seat. It was a relief to hear that I wouldn't be slowed down by having to deal with any of Zana's unimportant human worries. "How can we stop humans fighting? I stopped you and Saira fighting last time I was here, so I just need to do that again, for everyone on the planet. How long do you think that will take?"

Zana folded her arms. "Me and Saira weren't *fighting*. We just had a little misunderstanding.

And I'm not sure it was you who fixed that. Anyway, before you can start fixing the planet, we need to get you registered at school. Because my mum and dad definitely won't let me hang out with you if you're skiving."

To show how annoyed I was at this, I made one of my favourite sounds I'd learnt last time I was on Earth – apparently they called it "blowing a raspberry", although it didn't involve any fruit. The old lady sitting in front of us tutted and moved seats.

We got off the bus and walked through the school gates, where Zana hurried me away from the bustling playground and into the main school building. I followed her to the door marked COMPUTER LAB. It was secured with heavy metal bolts. Zana put her hands on her hips and huffed.

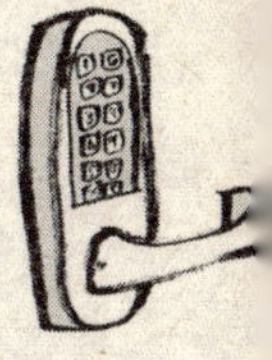

"I.T. have increased the security since I programmed all the computer speakers to play birdsong on a constant loop at top volume. Honestly, it's like the teachers here don't care that we're losing touch with nature."

I jiggled the door handle. "Can't you hack it?"

I asked. I remembered Zana was very good at this.

"Er, no. It's a door, not a computer," said Zana. "Come on, we'll have to try the library instead."

We went upstairs and into a big room where all the books lived. I'd only ever spent time here for detention, which was like a lesson, only more boring and everyone was very cross with you. There were a couple of computers in the corner. Zana sat in front of one and started tapping away on the keyboard.

While I waited, I wandered through the shelves of books. I stopped in front of a section marked "HISTORY". I had spotted a chunky book with a picture on the front of people wearing shiny metal outfits, in the middle of a battle. I picked it up, hoping it might have some easy-to-follow instructions on how to stop humans fighting.

Zana appeared at my shoulder. "All done. You're officially enrolled as a pupil at Oak Lane." She saw the book in my hands. "Oh, now that's a good idea! Seeing as you won't listen to me when I tell you that fighting is a pretty hard human problem to stop, let me show you."

She took the book and flicked it open at a random page.

"A HUNDRED YEARS' WAR?!" I read. "I haven't got that long!"

My teacher had only given me until the end of the day to fix my project. Luckily, that worked out as about three weeks in Earth time. But that still didn't give me enough time to get involved in a fight for a hundred years.

"Sadly that's just one of the many battles humans have had," Zana explained. "Humans have been fighting with each other for as long as we've existed. You could even say it's part of our nature, to compete with each other."

"I knew I should have brought back the dinosaurs," I muttered.

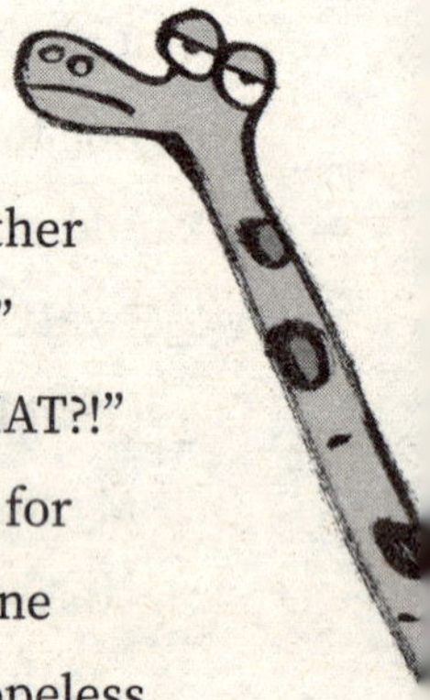

"Well, the dinosaurs fought with each other too," said Zana. "They even ate each other."

My mouth dropped open. "They did WHAT?!"

We were interrupted by the bell ringing for registration. I hadn't even been on Earth one whole day yet, and already I was feeling hopeless about my chances of changing anything. To make things worse, I was now going to have to sit through boring human lessons that I didn't understand.

When we got to the classroom, Ms Ashworth (a woman who everyone calls the Head even though she clearly also has a Body) was addressing the Year 6 class.

"And that is why we will have *no more* classroom hamsters until the pupil responsible for the parachuting incident comes forwar– AARGH!"

Ms Ashworth spotted me. "Sky Wall! What are you doing here? Didn't we expel you?"

Mr Martins, the Year 6 teacher, put down the newspaper he was reading at his desk. He looked at me, made a noise like a trumpet player falling down the stairs, put his head on the desk and put the newspaper over it. Perhaps he was pleased to see me?

"Sky enjoyed her foreign exchange here so much that she's joined us permanently," Zana explained.

Ms Ashworth went very still. When I'd last stayed on Earth, Zana had made me watch nature documentaries with her. Right now, Ms Ashworth looked like an antelope, the moment it spots a lion.

Eventually she said quietly, "No. Please, no."

"Yes," said Zana. "It's all official."

"But ... but ... you missed the start of term. I could expel you for that!"

"Sky was on a work experience placement," Zana explained. "You can check the system. It's all there."

Ms Ashworth snatched up Mr

Martins' laptop and jabbed at it angrily. "It says ... Sky was on a two-week placement as a rollercoaster engineer?!" she spluttered.

I didn't remember that.

"That's right. Sky loves rollercoasters," Zana said. She blinked at me using only one eye. I wasn't sure what that meant. Or what a rollercoaster was.

"Well, I don't recall seeing any of the paperwork on this pupil transfer. But it's all on the system. And I don't know how I can just kick a pupil out of the school." She leant closer to us menacingly. "But I *will* be looking into it. Until then, you'd better stay out of trouble."

Zana smiled. "She will, don't worry."

I was still struggling with human facial expressions, so it was hard for me to tell if Ms Ashworth looked worried. Although she did look sort of like the antelope on the nature documentary after the lion had eaten its leg.

Zana led me over to a table in the corner of the classroom, where three of our classmates were sitting. This was the rest of Eco Club, the group who had helped me on my last visit to

Earth – although, they didn't know I was an interdimensional being trying to save their planet, and it seemed a bit late to mention it now. There was Saira, who was the leader of the group, and the loudest (I hadn't worked out if these two things were connected); Arnold, who told me he was the brains behind the group (even I could tell this wasn't true); and Lucy, who probably wouldn't have been that bothered if the group didn't exist.

I thought they might be pleased to see me, as I'd helped save their school hall last time I was here. Although, I had also got their club banned for a while. Which might explain why they looked a bit uncertain, like a herd of antelopes trying to work out if I was a lion in disguise. (Maybe I had watched too many nature documentaries.)

The lesson started, and I realized that Mr Martins seemed to have decided to pretend I wasn't there. Whenever I spoke – to ask whether they had fixed the human number system since I last visited, or why there were so few elements on Earth's periodic table and when were they going to discover the one that slowed down time – he stared straight ahead in silence.

As we headed out for break time, Arnold tapped me on the shoulder.

"You're back just in time to watch my cricket match," he said.

"What's cricket?" I asked.

"It's a sport," said Zana.

"Never heard of it," I said.

"I imagine it's quite hard to play any sport in Antarctica," said Lucy. "What with all the ice. And penguins."

Lucy had a way of speaking where I couldn't tell if she was being serious or not. Sometimes I wondered if she'd guessed my real identity, and just didn't care.

"Cricket is the perfect sport for me," Arnold continued. "The cricket coach is a lot more appreciative of players standing round doing nothing than the football coach was. In cricket, they call it fielding."

"Don't you have to at least *try* to catch the ball?" Saira asked. She flicked her hair back. "That's what I'd do anyway. It's why I've not joined the team – I'd be so good I'd spoil it for everyone else."

"You have to *look* like you're trying to catch the ball," Arnold corrected her. "I study the batsman very carefully to work out where they're going to hit it. And then I make sure I stand somewhere else. I can't catch, but the coach hasn't noticed yet," he added proudly.

"Well, we're all looking forward to watching your match after school," Zana said.

"Good, because we need all the support we can get – we're playing Ash Road Primary."

Zana suddenly froze. "Actually, I've got a lot to sort out with Sky. I'm not sure we can come after all—"

"You HAVE to support me!" snapped Arnold. "Remember how I supported you when you did your sponsored silence? I gave you all my pocket money to stop talking."

Zana chewed her lip. "Fine. We'll come."

As the rest of Eco Club wandered out onto the playground, Zana pulled me to one side. "Sorry, Sky, we'll have to go to the cricket before we can sort out your problem. I'll keep thinking about it, though. Maybe there's something smaller you could fix?"

Zana paused. She was chewing her lip so much I wondered if she was eating it for lunch. Finally she said, "I should probably tell you something too, before the cricket match. You see, I've been having a bit of trouble myself with someone..."

Zana kept talking, but I wasn't listening. I had discovered that I couldn't listen and think at the same time, and right now my thoughts were bouncing around like a frog that had eaten too much sugar. Zana was right: I needed to fix something smaller. Because my teacher had only told me I needed to improve my planet. They hadn't said by how much. And although I couldn't stop every fight, if I could stop just one, it might be enough. All I needed was to find an easy fight to stop.

The only thing standing in my way was this game of cricket.

4

I'd seen a lot that I didn't understand during my time on planet Earth. Now I could add cricket to that list.

The whole concept of playing sport was new to me, and if all sports were like this one, I knew I wasn't going to be a fan. Zana had explained the basic rules: one team tried to hit the ball with a bat, the other team tried to catch the ball before it bounced. She had not explained why it was so boring.

The cricket match was against Ash Road, the nearest school to Oak Lane. I sat on the grass with Zana, Saira and Lucy, surrounded by other pupils and parents from Oak Lane, in our red uniforms. The pupils and parents from Ash Road were sitting in a separate group behind us, in their blue uniforms. Apparently we couldn't sit together because we were rivals.

"That means we hate everything about them and we have to beat them," Saira explained. "Although, we haven't been doing a very good job of that. They're brilliant at everything. They beat us in netball, football, tag rugby, tiddlywinks, swimming and basketball. We wouldn't even be playing cricket at this time of year if we weren't running out of sports that we haven't lost at. They even beat us at hockey, when I was on the team."

"Didn't they score the winning goal when you were taking out your mouthguard because you were complaining it made you dribble?" asked Lucy.

Saira scowled. "That's not true. They would have beaten us even if I had been paying attention. They beat us at *everything*."

"Hey, we might win the cricket!" Zana piped up hopefully.

"What, with Arnold on the team?"

Nobody looked convinced. Although Arnold

really was good at avoiding getting even slightly involved with the game. At one point he stood so far away from the batters that the man in charge, who Saira said was called the umpire, had to run over and bring him back.

Zana leant over and spoke quietly so Saira and Lucy couldn't hear: "You see, Sky, this is a great example of what I was talking about. Humans always compete with each other. It's part of our nature. There's no reason why our school should hate their school, and yet every time we play them at any sport, they turn into our big enemy. It's silly really, because everyone at Ash Lane is perfectly nice and—"

"Look at that stupid hair!" someone called from the Ash Road section of the crowd.

I looked at Zana. "I'm not sure that everyone at Ash Road is perfectly nice."

We turned round to see the girl who had shouted at us. She was wearing an Ash Road uniform and an angry scowl.

"Who has stupid hair?" I asked her. Most human hair looked stupid to me.

"Your friend is just as brainless as you are," the girl said to Zana.

Zana's lip was wobbling. "Ignore her, Sky. Heather is the girl I was telling you about."

I realized this was what Zana had been talking about when I accidentally stopped listening. I didn't ask for any more information. As usual, that didn't stop Zana from giving it to me. She had learnt that she usually needed to repeat things several times for me to remember them.

"I designed an app to organize bookings for the school hall," she continued. "Except I made a tiny mistake in the code and it scheduled Heather's karate club for two o'clock in the morning."

"I hope you're ready to lose at cricket!" Heather called from behind us.

I wondered if the game would end faster if we lost. If so, I was very ready to lose at cricket.

Saira looked over. "Oh no, is that bully here?"

"What's a bully?" I asked.

"Someone like Heather," Saira replied.

"Someone who tries to make their life better by making someone else's worse," Lucy explained.

"Someone who *fights with others,*" Zana added, raising her eyebrows at me.

I nodded, wisely. "I guess it's someone."

An Ash Road boy with curly hair trotted onto the field with a bat. It was Daniel, the boy who had helped us fix the school hall when I was last on Earth. He waved at us as he passed. "Good to see you back, Sky!" he called.

"Don't wave, Eco Club!" Saira snapped. "He's not on our team."

"Daniel, stop waving to those losers!" someone from Ash Road shouted. I was starting to think I didn't like being in a rivalry. It involved a lot of mean shouting.

"He's still our friend," Zana said to Saira.

Saira rolled her eyes. "For goodness' sake, Zana, where's your competitive spirit?"

Before Zana could look for it, there was a loud ***CLONK***

as Daniel hit the ball. The ball went spinning through the air...

Right towards Arnold.

Arnold was midway through a chant. *"Hit the wicket, catch the ball, cricket is such fun for all—"*

The ball hurtled down from the sky towards his head.

"ARNOLD!" screamed Zana. "CATCH!"

Arnold looked up. He squeaked. He ducked to the ground. He closed his eyes and stuck out his hands...

In the days to come, many things would be said about what happened next. Historians would debate it. (Or at least, we would debate it in our history lessons.) Eyewitnesses would argue about what they had seen. It would become known as the Catch That Changed the World (of Oak Lane and Ash Road).

Arnold stood up, holding the cricket ball triumphantly in the air.

"I caught it!" he cried.

"No you didn't," Daniel said. "It landed on the ground. I saw it."

"*I* saw him catch it," Saira called from the edge of the field.

"Did you?" Zana whispered to her.

Saira shrugged. "Not sure. I wasn't really concentrating. But it's a point for us if he did."

"That's cheating!" hissed Zana.

"That's cheating!" shouted Daniel, a lot louder. He turned to the umpire, a man with a very small moustache and a very big hat. "You saw it – he didn't catch it!"

"Er," muttered the umpire, tucking his phone back in his pocket. "Er, didn't he? I mean, it's in his hands, isn't it?"

"He's lying!" Heather bellowed from behind us.

Arnold was jumping up and down. "You're out! You're out!"

The umpire took off his hat and scratched his head. This seemed to help him make his decision. "OK. You're out."

"That's not fair!" Daniel complained, throwing his bat to the ground.

That was when the next unfortunate incident occurred.

When Daniel threw his bat to the ground, he was standing quite close to the Oak Lane bowler. The bat knocked the bowler's leg. The bowler let out a howl.

"HE HIT ME!"

The nearest fielder from Oak Lane shouted, **"Hey!"** and shoved Daniel. Daniel stumbled backwards and bashed into another fielder, who shouted **"Oi!"** and kicked out, which tripped up the other batter from Ash Road who was running over to help… **"Watch it!"**

Before I knew what was happening, the whole pitch was a flurry of arms and legs, of players pushing and shoving and running away (that last one was Arnold).

"Is this part of the game?" I asked Zana.

"No!"

I should have known: this was much too exciting to be cricket.

Spectators started joining in with the pushing and shouting. It was like someone had pressed a button to make cricket more interesting, but had pressed it a bit too hard.

"Oak Lane is as bad at playing cricket as Zana Jackson is at making apps," came Heather's voice from behind us.

"Wow, what a great insult," said Lucy.

"Wow, what great sarcasm," Heather hit back.

"Oh, this is awful," cried Zana.

I looked at Heather. I looked at the Ash Road and Oak Lane players. And, very slowly, like a cricket ball looping through the air, an idea arrived in my brain.

"This is a fight!" I told Zana.

"Yes..."

"Do you see what that means? I can stop this! I don't need the best grade possible – I only need to make a slight improvement. That means stopping *one* fight. Why not this one!"

Zana's face wrinkled, as the umpire ran past

us, wailing. "I'm not sure you've thought this through—"

I didn't hear the rest of what she said, because I was running too. I had a fight to stop.

"STOP!!!"

I yelled, bounding right into the middle of the field.

Which was when I got hit on the head by a cricket ball.

5

It turned out there was something even more painful than getting hit with a cricket ball, and that was sitting in Arnold's front room, begging him to let me stay at his house.

Zana's parents had made it clear, even to someone as bad at reading human emotions as I am, that I wasn't allowed to stay with them again. I was a bad influence. I unnerved them. I put things in the toilet that weren't supposed to go in the toilet, and had already ruined two of Zana's mum's scarves that way.

So we had to find another option. Unfortunately, that option was Arnold.

Zana used her negotiation skills (non-stop talking) to get us as far as Arnold's front room. Now

Arnold sat on the sofa with his arms folded and his forehead scrunched. I was sitting on the other sofa, trying not to breathe too loudly. Zana had told me not to do anything to annoy Arnold. As my existence seemed to annoy him, this was difficult.

"I can't have Sky to stay," Arnold said. "My parents would never allow it."

"Your parents won't even notice," argued Zana. "You've got four brothers. They can't keep track of what you're all doing."

Arnold's scowl stayed in place. "How long is she going to be here anyway?"

Zana shifted in her seat. "Just ... until she gets a good grade."

Arnold sighed. "That could take for ever. I've seen Sky in class. She barely understands numbers."

I shrugged at Zana. I couldn't argue with that. Humans only had half as many numbers as we had in my dimension, and I had given up trying to figure out how they worked.

Suddenly, a tiny human flew through the door and bounced off Arnold's head.

“That’s the smallest person I’ve ever seen!” I gasped.

“It’s not a real person,” Zana whispered. “That’s an action figure.”

I was about to ask what an action figure was when another one hurtled through the air and landed on Arnold’s lap. Another hit the wall above his head and another boinged on the sofa next to him.

Arnold picked the figure out of his lap. “STOP DRAWING ON MY STUFF!” he screamed.

There was giggling in the hallway, then four different-sized versions of Arnold burst into the room.

Arnold disappeared under a pile of legs and arms.

I gasped. "Fighting!"

Zana pulled me back before I could jump into the fray. "It's fine, Sky. This is what brothers do. Or at least, it's what Arnold's brothers do."

Eventually the four brothers let Arnold go. One of them paused to blow a raspberry (Arnold didn't seem to appreciate it as much as I did), and then they left. Arnold lay on the floor, looking like he'd ridden a kangaroo through a hurricane.

"Are you alright?" asked Zana.

"Yes." Arnold winced as he climbed back on the sofa. "They always gang up on me."

"This is perfect!" I cried.

Arnold glared at me. "How can my brothers ganging up on me be 'perfect'?"

I gave him my best smile. Arnold didn't smile back.

"I'm looking for fights to stop. I'm going to stop the fight between Oak Lane and Ash Road. I can stop your fight with your brothers. I might even stop Zana's fight with her bully!"

I turned back to Zana. "At this rate, I probably *will* get top marks!"

"So you've come back from Antarctica to be some kind of peacemaker?" Arnold asked. He glanced at Zana, as if he was checking if this was a joke. "But how are you going to stop all those fights, exactly?"

I hadn't thought about that part yet. So I smiled again.

"I guess," Arnold said slowly, "if you're going to stop all that fighting, you'll probably need to form some kind of club. Something like the 'Stop All Fighting Especially With Your Brothers Club'."

"Sure," I said.

"And I guess if you stayed here, you'd *have* to let me be in that club."

"Sure," I repeated.

"I do like a club," Arnold muttered to himself. "OK. Sky can stay."

"Thank you, Arnold! You won't regret this." Zana paused and lowered her voice. "Actually, I can't promise that."

After Zana left, Arnold showed me upstairs. His

room was only the second human bedroom I'd been in, but I was sure it must be the smallest on the planet. Despite it being barely big enough to fit any furniture, Arnold had crammed everything possible into it. Boxes spilled out from under the bed, more tiny little action figures crowded the windowsill, and a clothes rail sagged under the weight of everything hanging on it. It was lucky I didn't need to sleep in my human form – there definitely wasn't enough space for me to lie down on the narrow strip of floor next to Arnold's bed.

"This used to be a cupboard," Arnold told me, proudly.

"I think it still is..." I said.

"So," Arnold said, shoving a pile of books off his bed so he could sit down. "What's the plan? How are you going to defeat my brothers?"

I didn't want to tell Arnold that my one and only plan for stopping fighting had been yelling "STOP!", and that it had already failed.

"Er ... how do fights usually stop?" I asked.

"Well, the Awesome Squad end a fight by beating the bad guys." Arnold nodded at a poster on the wall behind him. It showed a group of impressive-looking humans in very tight clothes, flying through the air or staring into the distance. I wondered why their action figures were so small when on the poster they looked so big.

"Who are they?"

"Do they not show the Awesome Squad series in Antarctica?" Arnold pointed to the man in the middle of the poster with a billowing cape. "Captain Awesome is the greatest superhero of all time, and the Awesome Squad are his super sidekicks. My favourite is Billington." He pointed to a figure with glasses, standing in the background. "He doesn't have any superpowers himself. He's just sort of ... there."

I wondered if I should tell Arnold that I could see some similarities between him and Billington. I decided I'd better not, in case he changed his mind about me staying here. Instead, I asked, "What's a superhero?"

"You seriously don't know? Superheroes are people with special powers that make them better than everyone else." Arnold clambered off the bed and showed me the little figures that his brothers had been throwing at him. "Just look at them. They're *so* cool. Well, they are usually. They're not meant to have drool drawn around their mouths or BIG BUTT written on their back."

I held up the figure labelled STINK FACE. "So we need superheroes to help us end fighting?"

Arnold stared at me. "Superheroes aren't real."

I stared back. "Then why did you tell me about them?"

"I was trying to give you an example." Arnold snatched STINK FACE back. "To end a fight, you have to beat the bad guys and win."

I took a step back. (Or at least, I tried to. There wasn't enough room for me to do more than shuffle slightly.) I needed space to think. Arnold had quite possibly just given me the answer to my problem.

"To stop fighting..." I said to myself. "... I have to *win* fighting."

It was a start. Although not a very good one.

6

The next morning, Zana was waiting for us at the school gates.

"You survived!" she exclaimed. I couldn't tell whether she meant me or Arnold. Maybe both of us.

"Did Sky sleep standing up when she stayed with you?" Arnold asked.

"There was no space on your floor!" I protested. "I thought it was a pretty good solution."

"There is nothing good about me waking up in the night to find you standing in the corner of my room!" Arnold snapped. "I thought you were a burglar. Or a murderer. Or a burglar-murderer." He paused. "A burderer?"

"I know," I said. "You mentioned that when you threw your slipper at me."

We followed Zana into the playground. "I've been thinking about your plan to stop the fighting between us and Ash Road," she said, leading us past groups of pupils throwing balls and running round, as if they had no idea we were in the middle of a serious battle. "And I actually think that's a good idea. It's silly that we're enemies."

"I'm glad you agree, because Arnold has explained to me how to end the fight," I said.

Zana raised her eyebrows at Arnold. "Has he?"

"Yes. To stop the fight, I've got to win the fight."

Zana stopped walking. Then she realized I wasn't going to stop, and hurried to catch up with me again. "Hang on. That's not right. You can't stop fighting by doing more fighting."

"How do you know? I haven't even tried yet."

"Sky, there's better ways to—"

We were interrupted by the appearance of Ms Ashworth in the middle of the playground. She was waving her arms like she was trying to give directions to the birds.

"Emergency assembly! All pupils to the school hall immediately!"

Saira and Lucy joined us as we took our seats in the hall. It was the first time I'd been in here since Eco Club fixed it, and I was pleased to discover nothing was leaking or falling down. Most projects I was involved in didn't stay standing this long. It was a miracle Earth hadn't disappeared in a ball of flame yet.

Ms Ashworth stood at the podium onstage with her hands on her hips.

"Oak Lane Primary," she boomed. "Never in all my years at this school have I been so disappointed by the conduct of my pupils. When I was informed that a fight had broken out during the match with Ash Road..." She shook her head. "That's just not cricket."

"I thought you said it *was* cricket?" I said to Zana.

"It's a turn of phrase," Zana whispered back.

"But she didn't turn—"

"Shh!"

"This morning I have been on the phone to the headmaster of Ash Road," Ms Ashworth continued. "I have arranged for a delegation to be sent to their school to apologize in person. Do I have any volunteers?"

Arnold's hand shot into the air. He blinked at me with one eye. I wondered when I would discover what this meant.

"That's very gracious of you, Arnold," said Ms Ashworth. "Especially as I believe you were at the centre of the incident. Can we have a volunteer to accompany Arnold, please?"

Arnold blinked at me with one eye again. When I didn't respond, he grabbed my hand and put it in the air too.

Ms Ashworth looked straight at me, then quickly looked round the rest of the hall.

"Any volunteers?" she called. Arnold was jerking my arm side-to-side so forcefully, it felt like it was going to fall off.

“Anyone … at all … put your hand up … please…” Ms Ashworth desperately scanned the blank faces of the rest of the pupils.

“Ms Ashworth! Sky! Sky volunteers!” Arnold shouted out. For a moment I thought Ms Ashworth was going to try to ignore that as well, but at last she shook her head and sighed.

“Fine. I suppose it would get you out of my hair for a while.”

Saira raised her hand with such force she almost leapt out of her seat. “I want to go too, Miss!”

Zana was squinting at me and Arnold. She slowly raised her own hand as well. “And me!”

Lucy leant forward to look at us all. “Did I miss something? Is this meant to be an Eco Club outing?”

“Now, now, this isn’t a free-for-all to get out of morning lessons,” said Ms Ashworth. “If we send too many pupils it will look hostile. Arnold, Sky and Saira, you will go to Ash Road. To show that we come in peace, you will be accompanied by Miss Shepherd, our meekest teacher. Don’t take too long. Emergency assembly concluded!”

Zana grabbed my arm. “Sky. It’s important for you to know that fighting is *never* the answer. This is your perfect opportunity to end this fight by saying sorry. It’s so easy!”

This was exactly what I wanted to hear. I like things to be easy. Feeling positive, I joined Arnold and Saira at the school gates.

“This is our perfect opportunity to get behind enemy lines and win this fight,” said Arnold.

That sounded like the exact opposite of what Zana had said. I wasn’t sure if mentioning this would annoy Arnold, so I stayed quiet.

“What exactly are we going to do when we get there?” Saira demanded.

“Dunno.” Arnold shrugged. “We’ll think of something.”

Saira rolled her eyes. "I'd never have volunteered to join if I'd known this was going to be such a poorly planned expedition."

"All I know is what we're *not* doing," Arnold said. "We are *not* saying sorry. Do you think the Awesome Squad ever just apologize and shake the bad guys' hands? No! We won that cricket match fair and square, and Ash Road are just a bunch of sore losers. Right, Sky?"

There was only one thing I could do in this situation, the most clever, tactical move to ensure nobody guessed that I was confused. So I shrugged.

7

Miss Shepherd, the teacher who had been sent to accompany us, scurried the short distance down the road to Ash Road Primary School. She wore a cardigan that was too big for her and an expression on her face that I was familiar with when I approached humans: panic. When a plastic bag blew out of one of the bushes, Miss Shepherd screamed.

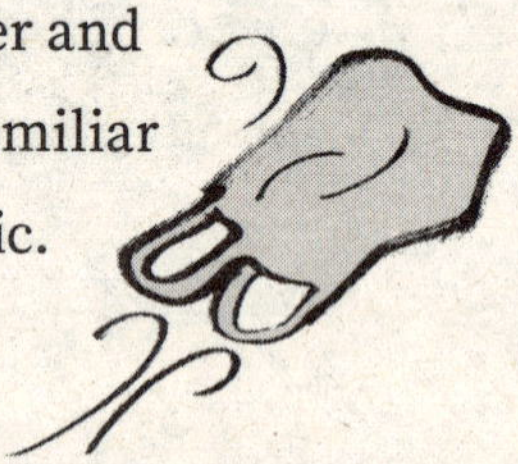

"Come on, children," she squeaked. "Let's be quick. I don't like being out when it's windy."

Ash Road looked almost identical to Oak Lane. The only difference was that everything was a lot cleaner and tidier. Oh, and there was a massive cabinet in the entrance hall bursting with gleaming trophies.

Saira bent down to read some of the labels. "Spelling bee ... national chess tournament ... hopscotch championships..." She tutted. "I knew I should have gone to this school."

"Well, I know one thing they're not going to win," said Arnold.

"Yeah," Saira agreed. "Next month's Knitting Showdown."

"No!" snapped Arnold. "This fight!"

"Oh, yes, that too," said Saira. She added to me in a whisper, "We *are* going to win the knitting, though. Anne in Year 5 has made the Leaning Tower of Pisa out of wool."

I didn't know what knitting or the Leaning Tower of Pisa was, but I did know that Saira liked it when I agreed with her, so I simply nodded and smiled.

"Children, please," whimpered Miss Shepherd. "Hurry along."

The receptionist showed us down a long corridor to a door with a sign that said:

HEADTEACHER

I frowned. "Is there a bodyteacher too?"

The receptionist heard me and pulled a face. "What are they teaching you at Oak Lane?"

We opened the door. The entire room was grey. There was nothing on the walls, apart from a picture of a grey animal that I recognized as an elephant. The headteacher was also very grey, from his hair to his suit, so it took me a moment to spot him in his grey chair, sitting behind his bright red desk. (Just kidding, it was grey.)

“Mr … Mr…” Miss Shepherd stuttered. She trailed off into silence. I decided it was time to practise being charming. Although most humans reacted to me with confusion, this was a chance to make a good impression.

“Hello, Mr Mister,” I said, smiling as big as I could. “Do you enjoy teaching heads?”

The man’s face remained like a stone. A big grey stone.

“My name is not Mr Mister,” he droned. “My name is Mr Pifflebackalack, and you have brought shame to my great institution of learning.”

“That name can’t be real,” Saira said.

Mr Pifflebackalack turned his stony gaze on Saira. “Mr Pifflebackalack is my legal name. I come from a proud line of Pifflebackalacks, stretching back to the time of the Vikings.”

Arnold raised his hand. “What’s your first name?”

Mr Pifflebackalack paused. “Ian.”

“Well that’s disappointing,” muttered Arnold.

“Children, please,” Miss Shepherd whispered.

I wasn’t sure when we were planning to tell Mr Pifflebackalack that he was a loser. Arnold looked a lot less brave now we were actually here, but before he could say anything, Saira did what she did best: taking charge.

"We're here to say sorry," Saira said.

Mr Pifflebackalack remained as still as a stone.

Eventually, Saira said, "So ... can we go now?"

"I am waiting for you to say sorry," said Mr Pifflebackalack.

"Technically we already said it." Arnold's muttering had shrunk to a mumble.

"Sorry for fighting at the cricket match," Saira snapped. "There. Are you happy?"

"Never," said Mr Pifflebackalack. I could believe that. "And your apology is inadequate. To redeem yourselves and the reputation of Oak Lane school, you must take action. I have a task for you to make amends."

Miss Shepherd had begun to tremble in the corner. "Oh no... Ms Ashworth didn't mention anything about this..."

Mr Pifflebackalack ignored her. He stood up, so he looked less like a stone and more like a big rock. "Follow me."

Out in the playground, he showed us a tall fence.

"We had this installed when our neighbours put a trampoline in their back garden. I found the sound of merriment, not to mention the visible bouncing, to be a distraction during my hourly laps of the school perimeter."

Arnold raised his hand again. "Why do you do hourly laps of the school perimeter?"

Mr Pifflebackalack narrowed his eyes. "To check for nonsense."

He pointed to a tin of paint by the fence. "Our caretaker has been taken ill today. The fence needs painting. You can do it instead and then I will consider you as having atoned for your misdeeds."

"What colour are we painting it?" I asked.

"Grey." Mr Pifflebackalack sniffed. I guess that should have been obvious. Especially as it said it on the paint tin. "You can find brushes in the art department over there. I will be passing by here in exactly thirty-five minutes during my perimeter walk, and I expect to find your task complete."

"Why does he talk like he's a dictionary?" Arnold wondered as the headteacher marched away.

“Maybe if we can speak to the bodyteacher, they’ll say we don’t have to do it?” I suggested.

“This isn’t a time for jokes, Sky!” said Saira, which surprised me, as I wasn’t aware I had made one. “This is outrageous. This is child labour. Are you really going to make us do this, Miss Shepherd?”

Miss Shepherd was breathing into a paper bag that she had been carrying in her cardigan pocket.

"You shouldn't have said sorry," Arnold said to Saira. "It's made everything worse. Exactly as I said it would. Mr Pifflebackalack is a horrible headteacher, which means his school is horrible, and so is everyone in it. We need to fight back!" He paused. "But first, you need to go and fetch those paintbrushes."

"You're not in charge, Arnold!" Saira snapped. "Luckily for you, I want to snoop round their school, so I *will* go and get the brushes. But *not* because you told me to."

As soon as she was gone, Arnold grinned at me. "I've just thought of a plan."

"Phew," I said. I always liked it when someone else did the hard work.

"We're going to write a message to Ash Road on the fence," Arnold continued. "Let them know this fight isn't over."

"Is that message 'We won the fight'?" I suggested.

"It doesn't work like that."

Saira returned with a handful of paintbrushes and another tin of paint. "Purple," she said. "We might have to paint the stupid fence, but it

doesn't have to be so boring."

At this point, Miss Shepherd also changed colour, turning from slightly pink to completely white. She dropped her paper bag, which blew around in the wind and made her scream, then stumbled over to the other side of the playground, where she sat on a bench and put her head between her knees.

"Saira, do you want to hear the secret plan that Sky and I have come up with?" Arnold asked.

"I've got a secret plan too," Saira said quickly.

"For what?"

Saira's eyes darted from side to side. "Tell me yours first."

"You haven't got one!" Arnold said, jabbing his finger at Saira. "We've got a plan *and* a club."

Saira folded her arms. "Oh? Well, *I've* got a secret club too. I guess we could combine them."

Arnold raised an eyebrow. "Really? Who's in your club?"

"It's secret."

"Is the secret that it's just you?"

As Arnold and Saira continued bickering

back and forth, I wondered if this was the start of yet another fight. They seemed to be springing up all over the place, no matter what I did to try to stop them.

I wasn't at all convinced that this painting a message plan was the genius idea Arnold thought it was, but it seemed worth a go. So I sighed, picked up a couple of paintbrushes, and pressed them into Arnold and Saira's hands. It worked to distract them from their argument. And to distract them from the fact that I was going to sit on the bench with Miss Shepherd instead of helping. There was no point me making too much effort, after all.

8

ASH ROAD ARE A BUNCH OF STINK FACES!!!

ALSO WE WON THE CRICKET AND YOU'RE **LOSERS!**

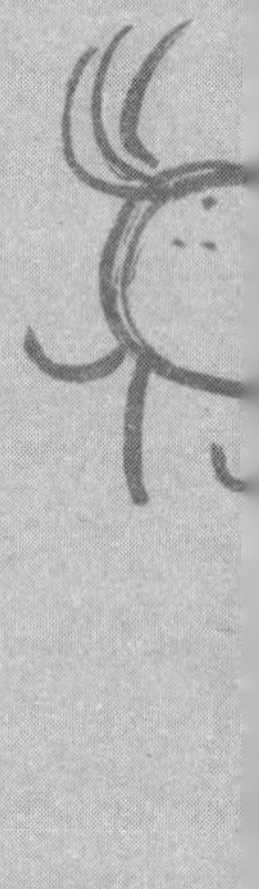

(THIS IS FROM OAK LANE BY THE WAY)

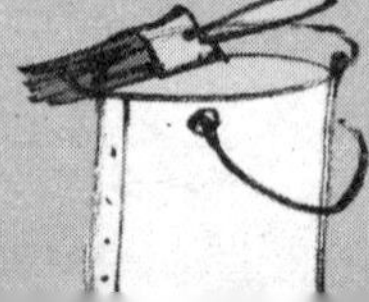

This was it: our declaration of war. Although Saira had also painted some unicorns round the edges, which didn't totally fit with our message.

We escaped Ash Road before Mr Pifflebackalack came back to inspect our work. Miss Shepherd was whimpering and making odd creaking sounds every time she breathed.

I felt great about our plan, right up until the moment Zana cornered us at break time.

"Did you say sorry?" she asked me.

I froze. The "Stop All Fighting By Beating Ash Road Plus Saira's Special Club That She Hasn't Just Made Up" Club had agreed not to tell Zana that we were continuing our feud with Ash Road. (Feud was a new word Arnold had taught me. He said it meant a long-running disagreement with an enemy, and that he had one with his postman.

Arnold had explained that even though she was our friend, Zana was not going to be a good ally in our project. (Ally was another new word. It meant someone who helped you even when you were making bad decisions. As someone who made a lot of bad decisions, I liked the idea of this.)

I thought carefully. "Yes. Saira did say sorry. At one point."

Saira nodded. "That's true."

"Oh!" Zana said, surprised. "Great. You know, I was so worried after what you said about needing to win the fight. I thought you might do something stupid."

"Are we really the kind of people to do something stupid?" Arnold asked.

I thought it was a good job that Zana was too nice to answer that question.

We decided to avoid Zana for the rest of the day, in case she asked any more difficult questions about our trip to Ash Road. The problem was we were in the same class as her and, as Mr Martins told me several times, I wasn't allowed to hide under my desk.

Somehow we made it to the end of the school day without giving anything away. Which was exactly the moment when a group of pupils from Ash Road turned up at the school gates and gave everything away.

"Oh look, there's Daniel!" said Zana, as we made our way across the playground. "You see, Sky? This is what happens when you say sorry. He's forgiven us and we can be friends again." She squinted as we got closer. "Although ... he doesn't *look* very friendly..."

Zana was right: Daniel was standing with his arms folded and his mouth scrunched up. Next to him was a scowling girl with curly ginger hair, a boy with long hair who already looked bored, and Heather, the bully.

We approached nervously – apart from Zana, who approached confused, and Lucy, who approached uninterested.

"Guys," Daniel said to the people he had brought with him, "this is the Oak Lane Eco Club: Zana, Sky – she's an exchange student from Antarctica, apparently – Arnold, Lucy and Saira."

"That's in reverse order of importance," Saira said.

"And these are my friends from the Ash Road Enviro Crew," Daniel said to us. "Alma" – he pointed to the curly-haired girl – "Elliott" – he pointed to the bored boy – "and I think you know Heather."

"Enviro Crew?" Saira snorted. "What a stupid name."

"Don't be rude," Zana said to her sharply. "What are you guys doing here?"

"As if you don't know!" Alma with the curly hair erupted, making us all jump. "Nobody calls me a stink face and gets away with it."

Zana turned very slowly to face me. She put her hands on her hips. She raised her eyebrows. I looked up at the sky and pretended I couldn't see her.

"What did you do?" Zana demanded.

"Nothing!" said Saira. She paused, then added to Enviro Crew, "What did you think of the unicorns?"

"Oh, were they meant to be unicorns?" said Heather, raising an eyebrow. "They looked more like sad horses wearing hats."

Saira gasped in horror. Lucy sniggered. I think she'd forgotten whose side she was meant to be on.

"Will someone *please* tell me what's going on

here?" cried Zana. "Who's a stink face and where did the unicorns come from?!"

"Your Eco Club graffitied our school and called us losers," said Daniel. "You're supposed to be my friends."

"And if you want to know who's a stink face, you should look in the mirror," Heather added.

Zana turned back to me. "Sky, I thought you said you apologized?"

"I said we said sorry. Which we did." I paused. "But we did also paint a message on their fence to challenge them to a fight."

"You were challenging us to a fight ... decorated with unicorns?" Elliott piped up.

"Everyone knows that's the universal symbol for a fight," said Lucy, which was news to me. Maybe Saira had been right after all.

"What kind of a fight?" Heather asked. "Karate?"

"Any fight," I said. "As long as we win."

"But probably not karate," Arnold added quickly.

"I thought you just wanted a cricket rematch," said Daniel. "After you *cheated*."

"We did NOT cheat!" squealed Arnold.

"Let's all calm down," said Zana. "This is getting out of hand."

"Just like the cricket ball that you didn't catch," Alma yelled.

"Watch it!" Arnold shouted back.

"Just like you should have watched the cricket ball instead of—"

"THAT'S ENOUGH!" cried Zana. That silenced everyone, although Alma continued scowling so furiously it was almost like she was shouting at us. Zana grabbed my arm and whispered, "Sky, you're supposed to be here to *stop* fighting. This is your chance. Help me stop this ridiculousness!"

"I am stopping this," I said. "By winning the fight."

Zana shook her head. I shook mine back.

"You better get out of here," Saira said to the Enviro Crew.

"Fine," snapped Heather. "But we'll be back. When you least expect it."

And with that, the Enviro Crew walked off down the road. (Alma somehow managed to walk off backwards, so that she could maintain scowling eye contact the whole way. It was quite impressive.)

"We shouldn't have done that," said Saira.

"I agree," said Zana. "Fighting never solves anything—"

"No," Saira interrupted. "I mean we shouldn't have told them to leave. We were meant to be leaving. It's home time. We can't follow them."

"Just stand here and look menacing," said Arnold.

So we did.

When we finally made it home, Arnold and I ran straight up to his room. Arnold said there was no time to waste. If only he'd had this attitude earlier, we might have avoided the cricket match.

"Did you hear what Enviro Crew said?" Arnold asked me.

"I heard it," I confirmed. I wasn't sure I remembered it. Thankfully Arnold did.

"They said *we'll be back*." Arnold's eyes went wide. "We need to protect ourselves! We need defences! We need to make Oak Lane into a fortress."

"What's a fortress?"

"You know, like a castle." Arnold leant over the edge of his bed and dragged a box out from underneath. He rummaged through it and pulled out a chunky book. On the cover was a huge building, with towers that had jagged stone teeth on top and shiny men guarding the doors. It was a kind of building that looked vaguely familiar from the Earth history videos I'd watched.

"Me and my dad visited lots of castles for medieval battle re-enactments when I was little," Arnold continued. "Dad always liked sitting quietly on the ramparts. For hours."

"And you want us to turn our school into one of those?" I remembered how long it had taken to turn the falling-down school hall into a slightly-less-falling-down school hall. This was starting to sound like a lot more work than I was prepared to do.

"That might be a bit ambitious," said Arnold. "But we can borrow some ideas for the defences. Like the moat and drawbridge." He pointed to a narrow river that looped round the castle. "These platforms are called machicolations and they're for dropping stuff on attackers, then there's a dungeon..."

"Hmm, interesting," I said. This is what I had learnt that human adults said when they disagreed with you and wanted you to forget whatever terrible idea you'd just had, but couldn't be bothered to argue. I didn't want to argue with Arnold, but I also didn't want to build a castle. Zana understood that I preferred plans involving minimal effort, and Arnold's ideas sounded like the exact opposite.

We were interrupted by a loud rumbling. The house shuddered around us.

"That's the dinner stampede," Arnold said. "Come on, before they eat everything!"

Dinner at Arnold's house was very different to dinner at Zana's. For a start, there weren't enough chairs, so his mum and dad ate their portions standing in the kitchen. No one asked who I was. From what I could tell, this was because talking would take up valuable mouth-time, which was better spent chewing food. Any hesitation risked losing a forkful from your plate to one of Arnold's brothers. Not that I minded – human food usually gave me a worrying amount of gas.

Eventually, when every morsel had been licked off every plate, Arnold's smallest brother wiped his mouth with the back of his hand and pointed at Arnold.

"Heard you started a fight with Ash Road."

Arnold's eyes darted across to his parents, but they were busy clearing up and weren't listening. Arnold nodded.

"Good," said his brother. Seeing as no one was telling me anyone's name (and I wouldn't have remembered anyway), I decided to number the brothers in my head. The littlest, Brother 1, continued, "I was so excited when I got picked as goalie for the Year 4 football team, and then we got beaten 11-0 by Ash Road in our first match. In the end I just sat down and read my comic, because nothing I did made any difference."

"It was the same when I was at Oak Lane," said Brother 4, the biggest one. "I'm so relieved I don't have to face them anymore."

"You know why they're so good at everything, right?" said Brother 2, who confusingly looked almost identical to Brother 1, right down to their matching pairs of glasses. "It's because of their headteacher, Mr Pyjamas or whatever his name is."

"Yeah," agreed Brother 3. "The robot headteacher!"

"He's a robot?" I gasped. I'd seen these on television, and it was true that they didn't look so different from Mr Pifflebackalack.

"Of course! That's why he's grey – 'cos he's made of metal!" cried Brother 4.

The brothers started making *bloop bleep* noises and jerking their arms around.

"They're just messing with you, Sky. He's not really a robot," Arnold muttered. I wasn't so sure. He *was* very grey.

"So, how are you going to beat Ash Road?" asked Brother 1, when they all finally got tired of doing their robot impressions.

"We're making a castle," Arnold replied quickly.

"We haven't agreed on a plan," I corrected him.

"Well, we can help spread the fight to our year groups," said Brother 2.

"And whatever you do, make sure you don't lose," said Brother 3, as they all got up from the table with a noisy scraping of chairs. "We're all counting on you."

Arnold puffed his chest out and smiled.

"Oh, and by the way, we threw your action figures onto the roof of the shed," added Brother 4.

Arnold's chest deflated. The four brothers scampered away, leaving me and Arnold at the table.

"Isn't this great, Sky?"

“Is the roof really a good place to keep your action figures?”

“Not that! This rivalry with Ash Road is the first thing me and my brothers have agreed on. I can’t remember the last time we had a conversation when one of them didn’t have me in a headlock.”

I hesitated. Arnold was grinning, but I had the ache in my head that I got when I was trying to work something out. “They said they were going to spread the fight to other year groups. Do we want them to do that? If the fight gets bigger, isn’t it going to be harder to stop?”

“Sky, I only let you stay here because you said you were going to help stop my brothers ganging up on me,” said Arnold. “This fight with Ash Road could finally be the way to do it!”

I scratched my head, in case this helped my thoughts untangle. "So you're saying, I can stop a fight – between you and your brothers – by getting involved in an even BIGGER fight between the schools?"

"Exactly!" Arnold patted me on the shoulder. "You stop fighting by fighting. Now, stop worrying and come and help me work out how to build a drawbridge."

As we got up from the table, Arnold's dad came through from the kitchen. His gaze caught on me. He stared, like he was trying to work out whether I was a daughter he had forgotten about.

"This is Sky, my friend from school. You said she could come for dinner," Arnold said breezily.

"Right…" his dad muttered, narrowing his eyes.

"We're going to build a castle."

"OK…" his dad said. Then he shook his head. "Wait!"

We froze in the kitchen doorway.

"Don't make any mess," his dad said. He sighed. "I hate mess."

10

That night at Arnold's was even more painful than the night he threw his slipper at me. This was because I spent it thinking – something I usually avoided at all costs. What I was thinking was that I needed to talk to Zana. I was wondering if she had a point about apologizing to Ash Road. It sounded a lot easier than Arnold's plans, which were starting to feel out of control.

So when we arrived at school the next morning, and Arnold said we needed to go and inspect the ground for the moat, I said I'd catch him up in a minute. Instead, I headed straight for the blue-haired figure by the school hall.

"Good morning, Sky," said Zana. She was inspecting the bug hotel that Eco Club had made.

"I'm worried there's been a dispute between the earwigs and the spider on the top floor," she explained.

"Not more fighting," I sighed.

"Ah, yes, I did want to talk to you about that," said Zana. "I'm not happy about your plan to fight Ash Road. It's not going to end well."

"I'm starting to think you might be right," I admitted. "Arnold keeps telling me that if we win the fight everything will be fine. But when does Arnold ever win at anything?"

Zana stuck out a finger to help a ladybird clamber off the hotel roof. "I'm glad you're seeing sense," she said. I looked round, but I couldn't see any sense. Maybe she meant the fence. "Because I've been thinking about how to help you."

"Excellent," I said, relieved. "I'll do anything. Well, not anything. In fact, I'd prefer to do almost nothing."

"I know," said Zana. She stepped away from the hotel and put her hands on her hips, so I could tell she was entering Serious Mode. "So, you know I think we need to apologize to Ash Road.

But sometimes it's not just about saying sorry, it's about *showing* how sorry you are. Actions speak louder than words."

"Is that why Mr Martins told me to stop hitting the big drums in music class when he was trying to talk?" I asked.

"It's a metaphor – look, that doesn't matter. I have an idea for how we can unite our two schools, overcome our differences and help you improve your project."

"That sounds perfect!" I cried.

"I hope so. And I'll tell you all about it. Just as soon as I tell you the bad news."

"Oh no," I groaned. "Who else are the earwigs fighting with?"

Zana shook her head. "It's not about that. It's Ms Ashworth. She wants to see you in her office."

"Oh no," I groaned even louder.

Zana guided me by the elbow towards the main school building. We passed Lucy coming out of the art room, carrying a bag labelled "CLAY". She waved at us, and didn't seem the slightest bit surprised to see me heading towards the Head's office.

"Come on, Sky, it'll be OK," Zana reassured me. "Just remember what I said: there is another way."

I stopped by the door. "There is? But I thought Ms Ashworth's office was just through here?"

"I mean another way to solve— You know what, it doesn't matter."

Zana left me in the corridor. A boy I remembered from my last visit to Earth called Rude Jaden was slouching on one of the chairs outside the Head's office, scuffing his feet on the floor. Zana had told me that Rude Jaden got in trouble so often, he had a season ticket to detention. (She then had to explain to me what a season ticket was, which she was annoyed about, as she said it spoiled her joke.)

"What are you here for?" I asked him.

"I put bubble mixture in the toilets," Rude Jaden replied. "Thought it would look cool when someone flushed them, but the school nurse said he had loads of people coming to him worried that they were weeing bubbles. What about you?"

"I painted a declaration of war on a fence."

Rude Jaden nodded. "Respect."

I knocked on the office door and went inside. Saira and Arnold were already there – Ms Ashworth must have captured him before he could start digging the moat. The Head was holding an ice pack to her ear.

“Ah, here’s the final member of the so-called peacekeeping mission,” she barked. “Take a seat.”

I tried to take Arnold’s, until he nudged me into an empty chair instead.

“I have just been on the end of an absolute ear-bashing from the headteacher of Ash Road,” said

Ms Ashworth, lowering the ice pack and rubbing her ear. "He phoned me to tell me what you three did to his fence. I suppose this at least explains why Miss Shepherd went home early in tears yesterday."

"How did he bash your ear through the phone?" I asked.

The rest of Ms Ashworth's face went as red as her ear. "I mean he shouted at me, Sky. Would you like me to demonstrate shouting?"

"No thank you," I said.

"Ms Ashworth," Saira piped up, "I'd just like to point out that painting that message on the fence was Arnold's idea."

Arnold spluttered. "Oh, really? I thought you were in charge of everything?"

"Don't let them get started arguing," I advised Ms Ashworth. "They go on for ever."

"ENOUGH, all of you!" Ms Ashworth erupted. It seemed she was giving us a demonstration of shouting after all. "You're all in detention." I raised my hand. "What, Sky?"

"Should I get a season ticket?"

"GET OUT!"

11

We all returned to the Year 6 classroom, along with Rude Jaden, who was pleased he would have some company in detention later. Mr Martins was reclining in his chair with his newspaper over his face. Zana was waiting for me. She looked at Saira and Arnold's furious expressions, and then at me.

"I take it that didn't go very well?" she asked.

"We're all in detention," I replied. "Apparently Mr Pifflebackalack was quite annoyed about the fence."

"I'm not surprised," Zana said. "Still, now that's out of the way, I can tell you about my brilliant plan. Because you did something really bad with the fence, you need to do something really good to make up for it. That way, it'll even out, and you can make peace – just like you want! So I was thinking about what we could do, and I had this idea, which is that–"

"PAAAAAARRRPPPPPPPP."

The room went silent. Mr Martins sat up.

"Children," he said, "I don't know where that noise came from, but it was not me–"

"PLUUUBBBBFFFFFTTTTTT."

Mr Martins was drowned out by a noise like the one my digestive system made when it came into contact with too many vegetables. The class started to giggle.

"Who is responsible–"

"FAAAAARRRRTTTTTT!"

That last one was just someone yelling the word fart, rather than a realistic sound effect.

Zana looked round the room. "Where is that coming from?"

From the desk behind me, Arnold hissed, "It's Ash Road!"

"I don't think they could be loud enough for us to hear from all the way down the road," I said. Even during my worst encounters with aubergine, the gas was never this bad.

The classroom door burst open and Ms Ashworth fell through it. "Is anyone else hearing this—"

"BUUUUUMMMMMMMMM!"

The classroom erupted in laughter.

"This is the best day ever!" Rude Jaden whooped.

"Cover your ears, children!" Ms Ashworth cried.

Arnold jumped out of his seat and crept round the edge of the classroom, opening cupboards and pulling out drawers.

"Aha!" he shouted, pulling out a mobile phone with a glowing screen. He jabbed a button and *"POOOOOO—"* was cut off mid-word, so we never found out what they were going to say.

"What have you got there?" Ms Ashworth snatched the phone out of his hand. "Was one detention not enough for you?"

"This wasn't us – it's Ash Road!" Arnold protested.

"A likely story. At least we've found the source of the—"

"SAUSSSAAAGGGEEESSSS!!!"

boomed down the corridor.

"Oh no you don't!" Ms Ashworth sprinted out of the room.

"At least they're running out of ideas for words," said Lucy, rolling her eyes.

"Come on, Sky!" Arnold grabbed my arm and dragged me down the corridor after Ms Ashworth. Zana and Saira ran after us. Lucy did not.

"BOTTTOOOMMMMSSSSS!"

Ms Ashworth skidded to a halt, then dashed down a corridor to the left. We followed.

"Why are we following her?" I panted.

"Because we're not getting blamed for this!" Arnold cried. "This was a dastardly plan by Ash Road to—"

Arnold never finished his sentence, because at that moment we all clattered into the back of Ms Ashworth. The woman I knew as I.T. had burst out of her office, right at the moment we were running past it.

"CODE INDIGO!" she yelled at Ms Ashworth.

Ms Ashworth staggered to her feet, grimacing. "I have already told you, I am not learning code names for everything."

"I sent round an email last week about this. Code names will save us so much time in emergencies," I.T. replied.

"We are in an emergency now. And we are wasting time talking about code names!" Ms Ashworth cried.

"ROTTEN EGGSSSSSS!!!!!"

I.T. turned and saw me. She raised a trembling finger.

"*You*," she hissed, pointing at me. "I thought you were gone for good!"

"I'm as disappointed as you are to find myself back on this planet." I paused. "I mean, school."

She moved her jabbing finger across to Zana.

"And *you*. This another one of your pranks, eh? First you make the speakers play constant birdsong, now rude insults!"

"SMELLY BREATH!!!!!!!"

"This is nothing to do with me!" objected Zana.

"Stop throwing accusations around and find the source of this noise," Ms Ashworth ordered I.T.

I.T. raised an eyebrow at her. "And how do you expect me to do that?"

"I don't know. You're supposed to be the I.T. expert! Triangulate the signal, or something?"

I.T. folded her arms. "You know, if you'd just give me permission to activate Code Indigo protocol..."

"Forget it!" Ms Ashworth set off running again. For want of a better idea, we followed her, Arnold trailing some distance behind as he tried to catch his breath.

"This isn't over!" I.T. called after us.

Ms Ashworth stopped outside the door to the staff room.

"YOU SUCK!" came through the door.

"Gotcha," she smirked.

Ms Ashworth disappeared inside. I went to follow her, but Saira grabbed my arm.

"We can't go in there," she said, shaking her head. "I'm not getting into any more trouble.

I don't have time for more detentions – not with my busy social life."

Saira flounced back towards the classroom. I was about to follow her, but Zana grabbed my arm. I wondered if I should start announcing where I was going before I moved, to stop all this grabbing.

"Sky, listen, we haven't got much time!" Zana said, speaking even more quickly than usual. Arnold was getting closer, complaining about having a stitch. Whatever that was. "Do you see, Sky? This is why we need my peace-making plan! If we keep fighting, things are going to keep escalating until someone gets hurt." She pulled me a little further down the corridor and lowered her voice, as Arnold staggered nearer. "Look, my brilliant idea is for a joint bring-and-buy sale between our schools on Saturday. I want to raise money for the gorilla sanctuary, and I know Heather needs to raise money to buy a tandem bike. She convinced her parents to get rid of their car to help the planet, but now her mum has no way to get her to her karate competitions. This fundraising event would benefit both of us and promote unity and understanding."

"I don't understand most of those words."

"All you need to understand is that this bring-and-buy sale will let us work together, get to know each other, maybe even make friends. That's how we solve the problem, Sky. You're never going to end a fight by fighting more."

Arnold stumbled up to us. "You guys run so fast!"

Ms Ashworth burst out of the staff room door, holding a mobile phone triumphantly. "Got it!" she declared, jabbing a button to silence it. "There will be no more bottoms on my watch."

"Ms Ashworth, I hope you can see that this wasn't any of us," said Zana. "We're all right here, so how could we have made the calls? It must be a prank by Ash Road as revenge for the fence graffiti."

Ms Ashworth clenched the phone in her fist. "And to think their snooty headteacher dared to tell ME how to discipline MY pupils, when HIS lot are even worse! Sky, Arnold, consider your detention CANCELLED!"

She disappeared back into the staff room and slammed the door.

"Looks like Ash Road actually did you a favour," said Zana. "Come on, we need to get back to class." She hurried off back down the corridor.

"I need a minute," Arnold panted, sliding down to sit on the floor. He looked up at me. "Do you see, Sky? This is why we need my fortress-making plan! If we keep letting Ash Road get away with pranks like this, someone will get hurt. That's how we solve the problem. We're going to fight more."

Maybe it was the after-effects of the noisy phones. Maybe it was the fact that Zana and Arnold had just told me plans which were the exact opposite of each other. Whatever it was, my head hurt. And I still had to do an entire day at school.

12

I decided I had to tell Arnold about Zana's peace plan. I knew he'd be annoyed if he thought I'd been keeping it secret from him, and I didn't want to lose my place to stay.

Unfortunately, it took me a while to work this out. Lessons made my head fuzzy, and then as soon as they were over, Arnold had to go to his after-school chess club, while I sat outside and waited for him. Then on the way home we bumped into Saira, who was quite annoyed that we'd forgotten to tell her our detention was cancelled.

All of which is to say, I didn't make the decision to speak to Arnold until approximately one o'clock in the morning.

Even more unfortunately, I had forgotten the

very first lesson I learnt on this visit to Earth, which is that humans don't like being woken up in the middle of the night.

"GARGH!" Arnold garbled, after I'd nudged him several times in the ribs. He flicked his bedside light on and squinted at me, crouching next to his bed. "Do I need to throw my slipper at you again?"

"I just thought you ought to know," I said, "that Zana wants to organize a bring-and-buy sale with Ash Road."

Arnold sat up in bed. "What? No! Do you know what this means?"

I thought carefully. "Do you have to buy the stuff you bring? Or do you bring stuff and then say 'bye'?"

"It means we need to accelerate our plans. There's no time to lose. We have to be ready to strike."

Arnold threw back his duvet, pulled on his dressing gown and started grabbing all his books on castles. He paused, and said over his shoulder, "It means you bring stuff for people to buy, and you buy the stuff other people have brought."

"Why doesn't everyone just keep the stuff they've already got? That would save a lot of time."

Arnold didn't reply. We spent the rest of the night making plans – or at least, until I got bored and Arnold fell asleep with his head in a book, which was about ten minutes later.

I did wonder if I was doing the right thing. The

truth was, my mind was getting a bit muddled about whose plan would be the best, and most importantly the easiest. By the time the bring-and-buy sale arrived I'd have spent nearly a week on Earth, and I didn't feel like I had anything to show for it. But I didn't feel good about following Arnold's plan without telling Zana.

Zana was my friend. She told me this constantly. But, Arnold explained to me, there were some things you shouldn't tell your friends. Like if their haircut made them look like a giant mushroom; or if you were going to the cinema without them because they chewed popcorn too loudly and ruined the film. (Arnold said these were random examples and he actually chewed popcorn very quietly.)

And that was why I wasn't supposed to tell Zana that Arnold and I were going to use her bring-and-buy sale to get our revenge on Ash Road. Arnold told me that the sale would be the perfect opportunity for Ash Road to infiltrate our school and sabotage it further, and even though I didn't know exactly what that meant, it didn't sound good.

So we told Zana we would help run a stall at the bring-and-buy sale. But we didn't tell her about the rest of our plan.

On the day of the sale, Arnold and I met at dawn. Well, we were both sleeping in the same room, so we woke up at the same time. But that sounds less dramatic.

We had a rendezvous at our secret location at the school. "Rendezvous" was another new word I had learnt. It was what you used when you wanted to make meeting up with someone sound more fancy.

"Are you ready?" Arnold asked.

I nodded.

"Then into battle we go!"

We had to wait a bit before going into battle, because we were early and no one had arrived yet. We sat on the ground for a long time, as the sun came up. Eventually Arnold got out a Tupperware box and ate his breakfast. When the first people did start arriving to set up the stalls, they were in cars, and Arnold said there was no point attacking a car. Also, he was still finishing his toast.

I was starting to wonder if I'd backed the wrong plan. "We probably should have set off a bit later—"

"Shh!" Arnold interrupted. "Someone's coming!"

I looked up and saw a group approaching down the pavement.

"Hang on," I whispered to Arnold. "How will we know who is an Ash Road pupil? Nobody is wearing their uniform!"

Arnold stared into the distance with a solemn expression on his face. "We'll simply have to fight everyone."

We took our positions at our arrow slits. You may be wondering how we could make arrow slits in the walls of the school. We wondered this too, for a long time, until Arnold pointed out that the gaps between the fence railings looked kind of like arrow slits, so we should just use them.

We also couldn't get hold of any arrows, so we collected some twigs from the park instead.

"FIRE!" bellowed Arnold.

"Where?" I asked, alarmed.

"Not *a* fire," said Arnold. "Fire the arrows!"

"Do you mean throw them?"

"Well there's no point now. She's walked straight past us." Arnold pointed to the first attacker/visitor who was wandering through the school gates.

"Your instructions were confusing."

"Never mind. Get ready for the next one!"

Arnold and I flung our tiny twigs through the gaps in the fence. They bounced off the approaching enemy – two adults and three children.

"Was that an insect?"

"Was that rain?"

"Did those kids just throw something at us?"

"We've been spotted!" Arnold squealed. "RETREAT!"

We ran as fast as we could to the school hall, hurtled up the steps and—

"STOP!"

Arnold and I stumbled to a halt inches away from Heather. She was holding a giant vase, which wobbled in her arms as she backed away from us. "Watch it!"

"Careful, you two!" Zana cried, darting out of the hall doorway to help Heather.

"Hands off," Heather sniffed. "This is antique, you know. My dad's donated his most precious vases for this sale. I'm going to raise more money than the rest of you losers put together."

Zana tried to smile. "That's great – although, it's not a competition. It's meant to be about working together and..."

Heather walked off.

"You two are late," Zana said to us. "I've just finished setting up my stall of miniature remote-controlled robot gorillas."

Arnold blinked. "Miniature remote-controlled robot..."

"Gorillas!" Zana held up a tiny grey monstrosity with glitching eyes and bits of black felt falling off. "Aren't they cute? I didn't quite get the hang of the design in time, but I'm sure they'll be fine."

"Who is going to buy a robot gorilla?" Arnold asked.

"Anyone who wants a gorilla but can't commit to a real one."

I leant closer and squinted at the robot. I was trying to see if it looked like Mr Pifflebackalack.

"Come on – people are arriving!" Zana said.

We followed her into the hall. Elliott from Ash Road held the door open for us.

"Have you seen Lucy?" he asked us.

"Who wants to know?" Arnold replied suspiciously.

"Elliott," I reminded him.

"If you do see her, let her know my mum's got the pottery wheel ready," Elliott said.

"That's probably spy code," Arnold told me.

Heather was placing the giant vase on her stall, in the middle of lots of other vases. They were so fragile they seemed to shiver every time there was a slight breeze.

"My dad's had these since before I was born," Heather told us.

"And have they always been so ugly-looking?"

Saira asked, walking over from her stall.

"Saira!" Zana scolded.

"What? She said my unicorn drawings looked rubbish."

"We're not here to settle scores!" Zana reminded everyone. "We're working together for a good cause. And maybe, by the end of the day, we'll even find that we like each other."

"Whatever," said Heather.

"Zana, I think one of your robots has escaped outside," said Arnold.

"Oh no!" said Zana, and she dashed out of the hall.

"I didn't see it," I said to Arnold.

"That's because that was a clever ruse!" Arnold said.

"What's a ruse?"

"Just get up the ladder before Zana comes back."

I'd spent a lot of time in this school hall on my last visit to Earth, but I'd never been up on the platform above the entrance before. That might have been because the last time I climbed a ladder, I fell through the roof, so I was banned from going anywhere above floor level after that.

The platform was narrow and near the ceiling. Arnold said it was originally built for the lighting rig for school plays, but now it was mostly used by the caretaker to hide stuff he'd confiscated from pupils and told Ms Ashworth he'd thrown away. It was strictly out of bounds for pupils, but Arnold said we could ignore that rule, because the platform made the perfect machicolation.

Don't worry if you've forgotten what that word means. I had too. I was just following Arnold's plan and hoping it would become obvious later.

We peered over the railings of our platform and looked down on the school hall. People were strolling inside and inspecting the stalls. Zana came back inside and took up her spot alongside Heather.

"Ready?" Arnold whispered to me.

Directly below us was Saira's stall, where she was selling her sisters' most fashionable clothes, which she promised they had donated and she hadn't just taken from their wardrobes. She was holding up a long glittery dress. "It's never been worn," she was saying to a customer. "It was going to be my sister's prom dress, but it's yours for five pounds—"

A milkshake landed right in the middle of the clothes stall, spraying yellow droplets all over Saira.

Arnold and I ducked out of sight as a mighty scream came up from below.

"I thought we were meant to be throwing them at people from Ash Road?" I said.

"Have you ever tried aiming a milkshake?" Arnold snapped. "You do the next one, if you're so clever."

I picked up a cup and shuffled to the edge of the platform. Below us, I could see Elliott and Alma. I drew back my arm...

SPLAT!

"MY GORILLAS!" Zana's robots sparked and spun as milkshake splattered all over them.

I ducked back to Arnold. "You're right, it *is* hard to aim!"

"Let's throw together, then we can't miss. You go for Elliott, I'll go for Alma. 3, 2, 1—"

CRASH!!!

Both the milkshakes landed right in the middle of Heather's vases.

Arnold and I watched as every single one tumbled to the ground and smashed into a thousand pieces.

"SKY! ARNOLD! Get down here now!"

"Maybe if we just stay up here, she'll forget about us?" I suggested to Arnold.

He shook his head. "No chance. We'd better face the music."

"Sorry, Arnold, but I don't think she's going to sing to us."

We climbed down. Zana's face was red, and it wasn't from strawberry milkshake. "Why did you do that?"

"Are you familiar with the features of a medieval castle?" I began. The look Zana gave me was enough to stop me talking.

"We weren't aiming for you," Arnold said. "Sky just can't throw very well."

"You missed too!"

Saira and Lucy ran over. "What is going on?" Saira asked. "I hope this wasn't a plan that I wasn't involved with!"

"Yes, I'd like to know what's going on too," said Zana. "Because I thought we were making peace with Ash Road, and this looks a lot like you two trying to fight them."

Luckily we didn't have to think up an excuse, because Heather came storming over. Unluckily, she was even angrier than Zana.

“I knew this would happen!” she cried.

“You knew milkshakes were going to fall from the ceiling?” said Lucy. “That’s a very specific thing to predict.”

“I knew this was a trap!” said Heather.

“I promise you, I didn’t know this was going to happen,” pleaded Zana.

“I don’t believe you! I know she’s your friend.” Heather jabbed her finger at me. “And now you’ve destroyed my dad’s priceless vases.”

Lucy picked one of the vase shards off the floor. “This one says it’s from IKEA.”

Heather snatched it off her. “You guys are in so much trouble.”

At that moment, there was the screech of tyres from the car park. We all looked out of the door of the hall. It was a grey car. You can probably guess who was inside it.

“Why am I once again receiving reports of Oak Lane shenanigans?” Mr Pifflebackalack demanded, striding over to us. “It’s lucky I was nearby so I could come and stamp this out right—”

"Where did he go?" gasped Zana.

"Ah," I said. "That would be our moat."

13

Ms Ashworth removed her helmet.

"Once again, I am disappointed but not surprised to find members of Eco Club in trouble."

None of us who were sitting in Ms Ashworth's office said anything.

Ms Ashworth sighed. "It's the helmet, isn't it?"

"What's it for?" asked Arnold.

"Donkey riding," Ms Ashworth replied. "It's what I like to do on a Saturday morning when I'm not disturbed by troublemakers at school."

"Not horse–"

"Just donkeys," said Ms Ashworth firmly. "Now. Can we turn to the matter in hand?"

"That would be most sensible," said Mr Pifflebackalack. He finished drying himself and placed his grey towel neatly on the radiator. (Apparently he kept a towel in his car at all times "in case of water-based tomfooleries".) "This represents another serious act of misconduct by your pupils, and I would like to involve the police."

"For falling in a puddle?" Ms Ashworth blurted out. Mr Pifflebackalack's eyes went so wide I thought they would spring out of his head.

"This was not a puddle!" he spluttered. "It was a booby trap laid by your out-of-control ruffians! I could have been gravely injured!"

Ms Ashworth took a second to arrange her face, until her mouth looked suitably stern and was no longer wobbling with suppressed laughter. "Of course, Mr Piffleback."

"Pifflebackalack."

"Sorry, Mr Pifflebackalack. I can assure you we're taking this very seriously." Ms Ashworth levelled her gaze at me and Arnold. "Can you explain yourselves?"

"Are you familiar with the features—" I began. Arnold stopped me.

"It wasn't our fault," said Arnold. "It was the hole

the caretaker dug last year for the time capsule."

This was kind of true. There had been a hole into which the school had been planning to put a time capsule, until they discovered that Rude Jaden had replaced the recording of the school choir singing a selection of pop songs with himself making a selection of fart noises. The time capsule project had been paused ever since, and so Arnold had suggested we expand this hole into our moat. Unfortunately, I discovered that digging was very tiring and gave up after 45 seconds. Arnold lasted slightly longer, but still didn't have the energy to dig the moat round the entire school, so we chucked a couple of buckets of water in and that was that.

Technically it had worked, as Mr Pifflebackalack had proved.

"Don't blame the caretaker for this!" Ms Ashworth snapped. "You've embarrassed the entire school at a public charity event. You're lucky nobody was seriously hurt."

"I was hurt," Mr Pifflebackalack said. "And I am very serious."

"Please, Ms Ashworth, it was an immersive history experience," Arnold said quickly. "They don't have castles in Antarctica. I was just trying to teach Sky."

"You can teach Sky without throwing milkshakes."

Zana raised her hand. "Ms Ashworth, as the organizer of this event, may I say something?"

Mr Pifflebackalack wrinkled his nose at Zana. "*You* organized this event? Then I am not surprised it ended in calamity. What else could one expect from someone with *blue* hair?" He turned back to Ms Ashworth. "That would not be allowed at Ash Road."

Ms Ashworth sat up straight. "I'm sorry to hear that. At Oak Lane we believe children should be allowed to express themselves."

"And that is obviously why you court disaster," Mr Pifflebackalack sneered. "This attitude is exactly why I tried to prevent today from taking place. I said it would interfere with my pupils' precious time on a Saturday; time which should be spent doing homework, practising music scales, reciting times tables, and completing circuits for physical exercise. And just as I feared, now they have been dragged into your parade of indecorum."

Even Ms Ashworth looked like she didn't understand some of those words. She sat silently blinking, as if that was enough of a response.

Arnold jumped in. He clearly felt he wasn't getting enough attention, even if that attention was a telling-off. "If your pupils are so perfect, how come they set off those phones in our school?" he demanded. "They can't be that well-behaved if they're calling us rude words like that."

Mr Pifflebackalack spluttered. "What is this insubordination and mendacity?! My pupils did no such thing! I would never allow it!" He jumped out of his seat. "GET YOUR HANDS OFF ME!"

That last bit was my fault. While Ash Road's headteacher was distracted, I decided it was a good time to gently knock on his leg, to see if it was made of metal. Unfortunately, Mr Pifflebackalack noticed.

"I'm being assaulted!" he bellowed.

"Sky, what are you doing?" Ms Ashworth demanded.

"Testing whether he's a robot."

For the first time, Mr Pifflebackalack was no longer grey. He'd gone a sort of purple colour, and was coughing and stuttering (a bit like a robot short-circuiting, to be honest).

"This is absolutely ludicrous," he managed to choke out eventually. "Unless you want me to involve the authorities, I demand that you punish these ne'er-do-wells immediately."

Ms Ashworth looked confused.

"I mean the children," said Mr Pifflebackalack.

"Oh, right." Ms Ashworth cleared her throat. "Look, Sky, Arnold. I don't agree with everything Mr Piffle... Waffle ... Rack..."

"Pifflebackalack!"

"I don't agree with everything the headteacher is saying. But this was a very serious incident, and someone could have been hurt. I have no choice but to suspend you both for a week."

"And the blue-haired child!" Mr Pifflebackalack interrupted.

Ms Ashworth frowned. "I will not be punishing Zana. She tried to do something positive for both of our schools, and it's not her fault someone else messed it up. She's suffered enough – look what happened to her little robot gorillas."

Ms Ashworth picked up one of the raggedy-looking machines.

Zana blushed. "Actually, that one wasn't damaged by the milkshakes."

"Oh!" Ms Ashworth squinted at it. "Oh dear.

Maybe you should keep working on these?" She placed the gorilla back down nervously. "Sky, Arnold, don't come to school next week. Now please, leave me in peace."

We'd got as far as the office door, when Ms Ashworth called us back. I thought she'd changed her mind. I thought this for approximately three seconds.

"Clean up the mess in the hall before you go," she instructed. "It's been so lovely in there these last few weeks, since we got rid of the smell of sewage. Let's make sure it doesn't start smelling of milkshakes instead."

14

When I first arrived on Earth, I didn't think anything could be more boring than a day at human school. On my second visit, I had been proved wrong – watching cricket was much more boring. And now I'd discovered something even more boring than both of those put together: spending the day suspended at Arnold's house.

That Monday, we tried everything to make the time go faster. We took it in turns parachuting Arnold's action figures down the stairs. We watched YouTube. Arnold tried to teach me several different board games,

giving up every time because I kept rearranging the pieces to look nicer. We hid in the garden shed for an hour when Arnold's mum came home for lunch from her job at the library,

so that she didn't realize we were suspended. We got so bored we even did some homework.

And what made everything ten times worse was knowing that, back home in my dimension, my classmates would be having the time of their lives, surfing black holes and laughing at the thought of me, stuck here on planet Earth, the planet with the worst grade of all time. (My teacher had told me it was even worse than the planet someone made entirely out of lava. Apparently some very pleasant lava monsters evolved there.)

Things were so bad, I was tempted to give up and go home, to tell my teacher it was impossible to improve my planet even the tiniest bit, and accept whatever terrible punishment I was given. I even got out the glob of slime that disguised my trans-dimensional transporter and left it to charge on Arnold's windowsill. (It was lucky his room was so messy, so he'd never notice it.) I felt like I needed to have a Plan B. Though returning home early was such a bad idea, it was more like a Plan Z.

When the school day finally ended and Arnold's brothers returned home, they brought an extra person with them. Saira arrived at the front door, breathless and flailing her arms.

"You've got to come quickly!" she wheezed. "Immediately! Right now! No time to explain!"

"I have to tell my mum I'm going out," Arnold replied. "And get my jacket."

Saira scowled. "*Fine*, but hurry up!"

All the way down the road and on the bus back towards school, Saira refused to explain what was going on. All she kept saying was that things had "escalated" and that it was "a good job she was there to keep an eye on things as President of the 'Fighting with Ash Road' club".

"That's not a real club," Arnold argued. "And if it was, *I* would be President. I'm the one who got suspended, after all."

We got off the bus, bumping into Lucy and Elliott at the bus stop. They were both wearing aprons with some kind of grey ooze smeared on them. We didn't have time to stop and chat, though, because Saira was leading us towards the gates of the park that sat roughly midway between Oak Lane and Ash Road. She flung her arm out dramatically.

"LOOK!"

Arnold coughed. "What are we looking at?"

Saira rolled her eyes. *"The swings!"*

We looked. There was a big set of swings right in the middle of the park. There was nothing particularly interesting about them, apart from the fact that three pupils in the blue Ash Road uniform were sitting on them, chatting.

"Sorry to repeat myself but … what are we looking at?"

"You are looking at Ash Road seizing our territory!" Saira cried. "They always used to stick to their side of the park." Saira pointed to our

left, where there was a climbing frame and a slide. "Now they're gaining ground. Who knows where they'll end up?"

"The other side of the park?" I suggested helpfully.

Saira narrowed her eyes. "That's exactly what I'm afraid of."

"Maybe they just didn't want to sit on the climbing frame," said Arnold. "It's cold and hard to balance on."

"Yeah, right," Saira snorted.

"Are you sure you're not just making a big deal out of this because we didn't involve you in the milkshake thing?" Arnold asked.

Saira stamped her foot, like it was the grass that she was annoyed at. "How dare you! Look, you can ignore this if you want, but don't come crying to me when they claim the good benches." She pointed to the benches over to the right, closest to our school, where a group of Oak Lane pupils were sitting.

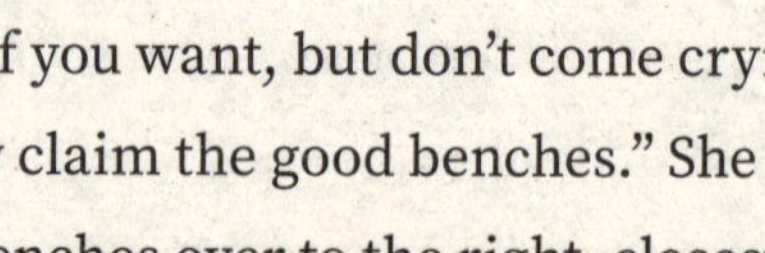

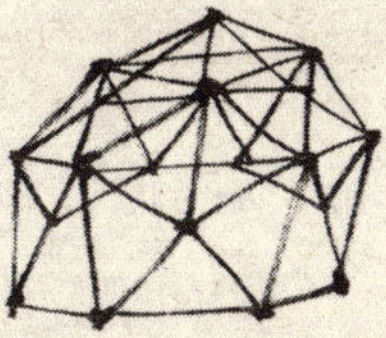

"They are good benches," I agreed. "And I do like sitting down."

"Sky, stop saying things," Saira muttered.

Arnold put his hands on his hips. "I think you're overreacting about the swings, but I guess we can't take any chances now we're in the middle of a fight. So, we need a plan of action: let's move the swings over to the Oak Lane area of the park."

"Don't be ridiculous," said Saira with a sigh. "All you need to do is come back here tomorrow and keep watch. Make sure they don't try to claim any more territory. After all, it's not like you've got anything better to do."

"That's true," I said, but only in my own head, because I'd been told to stop saying things out loud.

"I'll stop by at the end of the day so you can report your findings," said Saira.

"I'm not reporting to you!" Arnold snapped. "I'll report to myself, and if you're there to overhear it, that's fine."

We returned to Arnold's house in time for the dinner stampede. Arnold rushed upstairs and fetched a bowler hat and a woolly scarf.

"It's from when I played Charlie Chaplin in the Year 3 Nativity." He shook his head. "That was a confusing show."

"Why are you giving these to me?"

"Disguise," Arnold replied, wrapping the scarf around my shoulders. "You've been turning up to dinner every night for a week, and my parents are going to notice sooner or later. So from now on, we'll have to pretend you're a different friend every day, so they don't realize you're staying here. Oh, and don't mention we're suspended."

The hat and scarf definitely attracted more attention from Arnold's brothers. It wasn't enough to make them pause in their eating, though. Nothing could do that.

Brother 1 finished eating, let out a large belch, then said, "Heard you got revenge on Ash Road by chucking a load of milkshakes at them at the weekend?"

Arnold grinned proudly. "Yeah, we did."

"It's all anyone's talking about at school," said Brother 2. "Someone said you made some burgers into frisbees and knocked over all their stalls at the bring-and-buy sale."

I didn't remember that bit, but Arnold was nodding enthusiastically.

"I heard you're banned from every fast-food place in the borough because you're now known as the Notorious Milkshake Flingers?" Brother 3 said breathlessly.

Arnold did another of his one-eyed blinks at me. "Something like that, yeah."

"I heard you guys got suspended for it," Brother 4 said.

Arnold stopped nodding and started furiously shaking his head instead. "What?! No way! That's ridiculous. You know, you really shouldn't believe every crazy rumour you hear."

Now I was really confused. This was a feeling I was very used to, though, so I didn't mind.

"Well, whatever. You just better win this fight quickly," said Brother 2. "Because it's getting serious. Someone snuck into our classroom and messed with our displays. My project on World War Two now says it's on World War Poo."

"Yeah, you better not let us down. Don't ruin our family's reputation," added Brother 4. Then, to emphasize his point, he flicked a pea at us.

Arnold's brothers disappeared into the garden to kick balls around and roll on the grass and do all the other things that young humans find entertaining. I turned to Arnold.

"If the fight is getting bigger and spreading round the schools, isn't that going to make it harder to stop?" I didn't like the sound of that. "Maybe we should go back to the apology plan..."

"Shh," said Arnold, spraying his mouthful of mashed potato at me. "We can't give up now, Sky! It would make my brothers so mad, and you know what they're like when they're annoyed at me."

This was true. Last week they had put lots of marbles in Arnold's bed, so that when he got in, he rolled straight out again. I could see why he wanted to keep them happy.

Arnold's mum bustled over to gather up the plates and spotted me for the first time. Her eyebrows shot up in surprise.

"This is my friend from school," Arnold said

quickly. “Her name is ... Rye.”

“Are you cold?” Arnold’s mum asked, eyeing the hat and scarf.

“Actually, Rye is from Antarctica,” said Arnold.

“I...” Arnold’s mum shook her head. “I don’t have time for this.”

“See?” said Arnold, as she hurried out. “The disguise works.”

"Snacks?"

"Check."

"Binoculars?"

"Check."

"Vuvuzela?"

"... I don't know what that is."

Arnold put down his clipboard with a sigh. "It's what we'll use to scare off the Ash Road lot if we have to engage in hostilities!"

He picked up what looked like a plastic pipe and blew into it. It made a sound like a hundred angry flies arguing.

"See?" he said. "Perfect."

He shoved it into the rucksack we were packing, to take on our mission to the park. Arnold

had started talking like this a lot, mentioning "missions" and "hostilities". It made me worried. It sounded like he was enjoying fighting, rather than trying to win so that the fighting would be over. The one thing I wanted more than anything was for this to all be over so I could go home.

With Arnold's parents and brothers safely out of the house, we zipped up our jackets, saddled up the rucksack and marched to the bus stop.

When we arrived at the road where the park was, Arnold made us crouch down low and scurry along the walls at the edge of the pavement. He said it would stop people spotting us, but it was definitely drawing more attention.

"We should maintain surveillance from the bushes," Arnold said as we reached the entrance to the park. "That way we have the element of surprise over anyone from Ash Road."

Before I could reply, Arnold was scampering across the grass towards a clump of bushes around a bin near the swings. He attempted a forward roll, fell over, and crawled into the greenery. He waved at me to follow. I walked over slowly.

"Sky!" Arnold hissed as I crouched down next to him in the bush. "We're supposed to be stealthy!"

"There's no one here," I pointed out.

"There is," Arnold replied. "I spotted two dog walkers and two old ladies."

"Do you think any of them go to Ash Road?"

"They could be in *disguise*." Arnold took the binoculars out and poked them through the branches. "I'll be lookout."

"OK," I said, and closed my eyes.

"*You* can still look, Sky. I'm just the official lookout, which means I get the binoculars."

We waited. And we waited. Arnold said I wasn't allowed to talk, because it would give away our position, and also I was annoying him. At one point we were discovered by a friendly dog, and I got hit on the head by rubbish someone was aiming at the bin.

When we had been there for what felt like hours but turned out to be only ten minutes, Arnold said, "Everyone's at school."

"What?"

Arnold lowered his binoculars. "I shouldn't have let Saira panic us. I should have realized. No one from Ash Road is going to gain any territory until at least three-thirty this afternoon."

"What time is it now?"

"Twenty past nine."

"So how long is it until three-thirty?"

"You really need to learn your numbers. The point is, it's too long for us to be sitting here getting weed on by dogs."

"Did that dog wee on me?!" I wiped my sleeve frantically.

"Come on. I've got a better idea."

We clambered out from the bushes.

"We need to mark our territory," Arnold explained. "You know, plant a flag to show that these swings belong to Oak Lane."

Unlike vuvuzelas, I'd seen pictures of flags so I knew what one of those was. "Did you bring a flag?"

"No," said Arnold, unzipping his jacket. "But I brought my school jumper!"

He pulled his jumper over his head and tied its sleeves round the frame of the swings. The flags that I'd seen in pictures fluttered proudly in the wind. Our flag slumped sadly.

"That will do," said Arnold. "Let's go home before we get any colder."

Though the rest of the day at Arnold's house was warmer, it wasn't any less boring. Eventually his mum came back and we retreated to his bedroom. Arnold stood staring out of his window. He did this when he was deep in thought, which I knew because he'd told me several times.

"We need to get smarter," he said eventually.

"Tell me about it," I sighed. If I was smarter, I

could have avoided this whole mess.

"Our attack at the bring-and-buy sale was too obvious," Arnold continued, as if he hadn't heard me. "It's left us stuck at home, like losers. We need to be sneakier and bring them down from the inside. We need ..." Arnold spun round to face me. "... a mole!"

"Wouldn't a giraffe be better?" I suggested. Obviously I'd have really liked a dinosaur, but I was trying to focus on the best non-extinct creatures now.

"Not a *real* mole," Arnold sighed. "A mole is a spy on the other side. We need someone who goes to Ash Road to tell us what they're planning, so we can stay one step ahead of them."

"A friend?"

"We can't be friends with anyone who goes to Ash Road," Arnold reminded me, "because they're our rivals. What we need is someone who has helped us out before, who could be persuaded to help us out again. Someone like Daniel."

I thought about this. "What about Daniel?" I suggested. "He's exactly like Daniel."

Arnold scowled. "That's what I meant. Stop stealing my ideas."

The doorbell rang. Arnold's mother called up the stairs for us. We went down. Daniel was standing on the doorstep.

Arnold and I gawped at each other.

"Did we just wish him into existence?" Arnold muttered to me.

"Can you do that?" I asked. "I WISH FOR DINOSAURS!"

Nothing happened. I knew it was too good to be true.

"I think this is yours."

Daniel was holding up Arnold's flag/jumper.

Arnold folded his arms. "What makes you think it's mine?"

"It's got your name tag sewn into the collar."

Arnold snatched it out of his hands.

"You're welcome," said Daniel. He was looking at me with even more suspicion than humans usually did. "Why are you wearing a cowboy hat and a plastic moustache?"

"It's a disguise for dinner," I explained.

"That doesn't explain anything."

"You should come in and eat with us," Arnold said quickly.

"Really?" Daniel and I said at the same time. Arnold elbowed me sharply in the side and gave me one of those one-eyed blinks. I still didn't know what that meant.

Daniel's feet shuffled, as if they were trying to decide whether to stay or go. "I've been thinking ... we're supposed to be friends. In fact, we still are friends. This fight is stupid."

"Fighting is stupid," I agreed. "If it was up to me, there would be none of it on the entire planet."

"Right... I forgot how entertaining you can be, Sky," Daniel said with a smile. Then he shrugged. "Thank you for the peace offering. I will stay for dinner."

Arnold's brothers were all out, training for different but probably equally pointless sports, which meant there was enough room for everyone around the table. It also meant Arnold's parents had plenty of time to stare at me and my disguise.

"Remind me who these friends are?" Arnold's mum said.

"This is Daniel," Arnold said. "And this is ... Jai."

Daniel frowned. "This is getting weirder and weirder."

"Tell me about it," muttered Arnold's dad.

Once dinner was finished, Arnold led me and Daniel out into our secret base – or, as the rest of the family called it, the garden shed. I would have preferred a secret base without so many of the horrible stringy things called cobwebs, but we didn't have many options. Arnold's room was too small for all three of us.

"Take a seat," Arnold told Daniel.

Daniel looked round at the lawnmower, old paint tins and empty paddling pool. "Where?"

Arnold turned a bucket upside down. "There."

Daniel sat.

"Now that we have you here, trapped—"

"I'm not trapped," Daniel interrupted. "I could get up and walk out right now."

"No, you're our prisoner," Arnold insisted.

"I thought you invited me for dinner because you wanted to end all this stupid fighting?"

"We do!" I said.

"We do," Arnold repeated. "Which is why you've been recruited as our mole, to help us spy on Ash Road."

"No," said Daniel.

"You can't say no," Arnold snapped. "You're our prisoner. You have to agree."

"No, I don't."

"Stop saying no!" cried Arnold. I could tell he was getting angry, because his bottom lip was sticking out like it was trying to attack Daniel. Arnold gave me this look a lot. "We're going to keep you here in our dungeon—"

"I thought this was our secret base?" I said.

"It's now our dungeon. And we're going to keep Daniel here until he agrees to be our spy."

"No," said Daniel again, "you'll keep me in your shed until my mum rings your mum and asks why I haven't come home."

"Well then we'll put your mum in the dungeon," said Arnold.

"There's not really enough space for anyone else to—"

"FREEEEEDOOOOMMMMMMMMM!!!"

It was not Daniel who shouted this. It was not Arnold, and it certainly wasn't me.

A ginger-haired whirlwind burst through the door of the shed. Unfortunately, as the shed was quite small, Alma's dramatic entrance was immediately ruined by her tripping over the paddling pool.

"Your rescue mission has arrived," Alma announced, picking herself up off the floor. She had brown and green smears on her cheeks and forehead. "Run, Daniel!"

"I don't need rescuing," said Daniel. "There isn't even a lock on the door."

"How did you get here?" Arnold demanded.

Alma glowered at him. "Your mum let me in."

"You have something on your face," I told Alma.

"It's camouflage!" Alma scowled at me. Although, I'd never seen her not scowling, so maybe that was just what her face looked like. "And stop talking to me – this is meant to be a rescue. Come on, Daniel."

"Did you follow me here?" Daniel asked.

"Of course," said Alma. "You really think I'd let you go into enemy territory alone? I knew they'd take you prisoner. And I knew it was up to me to save you."

"But I've been here ages," Daniel pointed out.

"It took me a while to draw on my camouflage," Alma muttered.

"Well, my mum would have turned up eventually, but thanks anyway."

"I also came here to settle this fight once and for all." Alma jabbed Arnold in the chest. "I challenge you to a duel."

Arnold jabbed Alma back. “You’re on. Name the time and place.”

“Tomorrow. The park between our schools,” Alma growled.

“The one opposite the library?” Arnold snarled back.

“No. The one opposite the pet shop,” Alma roared. “Winner takes all!”

“All the pets?” I asked.

“Be quiet, Sky,” Arnold and Alma said together.

It was the first time I’d ever heard them agree.

17

I had got used to humans looking at me strangely. The looks Arnold and I were getting at the park, however, were beyond anything I'd experienced before.

It had taken a long time for Arnold to get ready for the duel, and an even longer time for us to get to the park. Now we were waiting for Alma on one of the benches on the Oak Lane side of the park – although Arnold wasn't able to sit down, so he was standing next to it. Everyone around us was either pointing, laughing, gasping, or in the case of one man, doing all three at once, which made him fall over.

"She's late," said Arnold, in a muffled voice. "If she doesn't turn up, does that mean we win?"

Before we could decide, Alma appeared at the entrance to the park. She was wearing her school uniform and carrying a box. When she spotted Arnold, she froze.

“What on EARTH are you wearing?” she shrieked.

Do you know what a duel is? Arnold and I thought we did. Arnold had showed me videos from the medieval battle re-enactments he and his dad used to go to, where knights in shiny armour charged at each other with sticks, sometimes while

riding horses, doing what they called "jousting".

Arnold didn't have a horse, and neither did the pet shop. (Although we didn't have much chance to look, as the lady behind the counter asked us to leave very soon after we entered.) Arnold said this was OK, as he was pretty sure Alma didn't have a horse either, so they could duel on foot.

The other problem was that we didn't have a jousting pole. That was OK too, Arnold had said, as he took the curtain pole off the wall above his bedroom window. This would work just as well.

The one thing we did have was armour. Arnold's dad kept his old outfit from the re-enactments in the attic. It was a bit big for Arnold, so we didn't bother with the legs. We put the heavy metal vest over his head and it almost reached to his knees. The helmet was twice the size of Arnold's head, and the little flap that was supposed to lift up so he could see better kept slamming shut over his

face. Arnold had to hold onto me all the way to the park to stop himself falling over or walking into walls, which I managed to stop him doing – apart from eight times when I wasn't paying attention.

What was strange was that Alma had turned up without any armour at all. And she was staring at us like *we* were the ones who had made a mistake.

"What's going on?" Arnold said through the helmet. "Is she here yet?"

Alma walked over to the bench. She placed the box next to me and opened it. It folded out into a board decorated with black and white squares.

"I meant chess," she said. "A duel ... at chess."

The suit of armour squeaked as Arnold looked round. "Who said that?"

"How do you duel at chess?" I asked.

"Chess?" Arnold repeated. There was a quiet "oh no" from inside the armour.

"I thought it went without saying," Alma continued. "Especially as we play so often online."

"Eh?" clanged the armour.

"Username ARAlma?"

"That's you?!"

"I thought that was obvious," said Alma. "The AR stands for Ash Road. I try out my tactics on you during our after-school chess club."

"I thought the AR was because you were a pirate," Arnold said glumly. The suit of armour slumped, letting off a metallic groan as it did so.

"So you're not going to joust?" I asked.

"Of course not," said Alma. "That would be ridiculous!"

"AHA!" shouted Arnold suddenly, making both me and Alma jump. "Obviously I knew you meant a duel at chess!"

"Did you?" I said, confused. "I'm pretty sure you told me that you were going to joust–"

"This was all a trick!" Arnold interrupted me. "The first rule of chess is to confuse your opponent! My plan has worked perfectly. Get ready to lose!"

"I don't mind waiting if you want to go home and get changed," said Alma. She sounded a bit sorry for us.

"I don't need to get changed because I didn't make a mistake," Arnold snapped. "Let's play."

"If you insist..."

Alma carefully set up the black pieces on her side of the board, and the white pieces on Arnold's side.

"You go first," Alma said.

With great difficulty, Arnold clanked closer. He lifted the flap at the front of his helmet, and looked at the board for about three seconds before it snapped shut again.

"Hmm," he said.

He leant over, reached for a piece, and promptly knocked everything over.

"That was on purpose!" Arnold said quickly. "Second rule of chess: do the unexpected."

Chess was one of the games Arnold had very briefly tried to teach me while we were suspended. He gave up because I kept picking up the board instead of the pieces, so I still didn't understand the rules. Despite that, I could tell Arnold wasn't doing very well.

"Maybe I should move the pieces for you?" I suggested, as Alma set up the board again.

"That's against the rules," Arnold pointed out. "And you'd be even worse than me."

So Arnold tried again. This time he managed to pick up one of his pieces, and he put it down again randomly. Alma took her turn and immediately captured Arnold's piece. This same pattern repeated on every turn, until Alma declared, "Checkmate!"

I glanced over Arnold. "Check him for what?"

"It means she's won, Sky," Arnold said. "Shall we play again – best of three?"

"As if!" snorted Alma. "I won this duel. And that means I've settled this fight – Oak Lane are officially LOSERS!"

"I didn't agree to that!" Arnold protested. "This isn't over! Just you wait! We're going to get revenge! You'll regret the day you messed with—"

"She's already left," I told Arnold.

"Chase her, Sky!"

As Arnold couldn't see out of his helmet, I figured he wouldn't know if I didn't bother.

You might think this was an all-time low for us in our fight with Ash Road. But it turns out there was one thing that could make it worse. And that was Saira turning up and laughing at us.

Which is exactly what happened next.

"Sky!" Saira spluttered through her giggles. "What are you doing? Please don't tell me that's Arnold in the armour?!"

"OK, I won't tell you," I said.

"Oh no." The armour seemed to droop. "Is that Saira?"

"I was checking out the park on my way home from school," said Saira. "Making sure Ash Road hadn't claimed any more territory. I did not expect to find you here. Especially not dressed like that!"

"It's not funny, Saira!" Arnold shouted.

Unfortunately the way the armour screeched and clanked when he got annoyed was quite funny, and it only made Saira laugh more. "We were trying to win the fight!"

"The only thing you're going to win is most embarrassing outfit of the year," Saira sniggered.

"Well, at least that's something," I said to Arnold. It didn't seem to cheer him up.

"Saira, you are officially kicked out of the 'Arnold's Awesome Squad to Defeat Ash Road' club," he yelled.

"Whatever," said Saira. "You're kicked out of my club."

"I didn't want to be in your club," replied Arnold.

"Good," said Saira. "Then I guess everyone is happy."

I still wasn't very good at reading human emotions, but even I could tell that this wasn't true.

18

I never thought I'd be so pleased to return to school, but after a week trapped at Arnold's, anything was an improvement. Word had spread at both schools about Arnold losing the duel with Alma, and it had not impressed his brothers. In fact, the fighting between Arnold and his brothers now seemed even worse than the fighting between Oak Lane and Ash Road. They'd put food dye in his dinner so he had to eat blue spaghetti (I didn't understand the problem with this, but it really annoyed Arnold); they turned the hot water off every time he went for a shower; and his action figures would never be the same again after we'd rescued them from the toilet.

Once we returned to school, it became clear

that Arnold and Saira were now also fighting each other. For someone who had come to Earth to fix the problem of fighting, I suddenly seemed to be in the middle of an awful lot of fights. And time was running out – I had less than a week left to stop any of them before my teacher would be re-marking my project.

"Welcome back, Sky," said Zana, as Arnold and I met the rest of Eco Club in the playground on Monday morning. Saira had her arms folded and her angry frown ready. Lucy was carrying some kind of orangey little vase and was looking quite pleased with herself.

Zana continued, "You'll be pleased to hear that you've been away long enough for me to stop feeling annoyed about what you did to my bring-and-buy sale."

"Sorry about your robots," I said. "Although, at least they weren't any good before they got covered in milkshake."

Zana's face couldn't decide whether to frown or smile.

"Just so you know, I'm still annoyed with *you*,"

Arnold said to Saira. "I know you told everyone about me losing the duel."

"Well, I'm *more* annoyed at you," Saira replied. "Ash Road are making so much fun of us because of that – and they've totally claimed the swings in the park as well, because you didn't keep watch."

Arnold and Saira stormed off to opposite sides of the playground.

"So great to have the gang back together," said Lucy. She sighed and wandered off in another direction for some peace and quiet.

"Sky, are you noticing a pattern here?" Zana said to me. "The more you try to win this fight, the worse it makes everything. You've been suspended, we've started fighting among ourselves, and Heather's being meaner to me than ever. She ambushed me on the way home from school last week and put a frog in my backpack. Luckily she didn't realize I have a deep affinity with amphibians and so was very excited by the opportunity to find a new home for it – but that's not the point. You need to stop this fighting. Which is why I've come up with a new plan for you."

"You have?"

Zana grinned and handed me a piece of paper.

"GORILLA TALENT SHOW," I read. "What's this got to do with the fighting? And what sorts of talents do gorillas have?"

Zana sighed. "You're not the first person to ask that. I knew I should have called it something different. It's not a talent show starring gorillas, it's a talent show for Oak Lane and Ash Road pupils to help raise money *for* the gorillas. It's the perfect way to make things up with Heather. She loves showing off."

“I don’t think I understand how this is going to help stop the fighting.”

“Of course it will!” Zana said chirpily. “It’s like I told you: humans love to compete. This is a way for Oak Lane and Ash Road to compete in a fun and friendly way, and to see that we like the same things and we’re not really enemies!”

There was no point arguing with Zana – especially as she’d already got permission from Ms Ashworth to host the talent show in the school hall on Wednesday lunchtime. She’d even got Daniel to hand out invitations at Ash Road, which was very good of him after the whole prisoner situation. And it wasn’t like I had any better ideas. Or even any ideas at all.

Our lessons that morning were made slightly more entertaining by Saira and Arnold’s feud. Every time one of them put their hand up to give an answer, the other one put their hand up to disagree.

When Saira said 4 times 8 was 32, Arnold quickly shouted that it was actually 40. I had no way of knowing which of them was right.

At break time, Zana and I positioned ourselves in between Arnold and Saira. Lucy positioned herself very far away.

"Would either of you like to enter the talent show?" Zana asked.

"I will!" Arnold said quickly.

Saira snorted. "What talents have you got?"

"I can find some," Arnold said defensively.

"I'll do my karate," said Saira.

"Oh, perfect," said Zana. "Heather wanted to do karate too, so you can go up against her."

"It's up to you if you want to put Heather on stage at the same time as me," Saira sniffed. "All I'll say is that one of us will definitely have all the audience's attention." She paused. "That person will be me."

Arnold whispered to me, "This talent show is our perfect opportunity for revenge against Alma and the rest of Ash Road!"

"That's not exactly how Zana described it," I whispered back. "She said this was the perfect opportunity to see how much we have in common and end the fighting."

“Yeah, right,” said Arnold. “This is our chance for the ultimate face-off.”

“Do we need to bring your armour again?” I asked him.

Arnold didn’t talk to me for the rest of break time.

19

The talent show had been scheduled for Wednesday lunchtime. As the Ash Road pupils streamed through our school gates, I wondered if I was making a mistake. Arnold was convinced we were going to beat them once and for all; Zana was convinced we were all going to realize we had more fun when we joined together. But we'd never beaten Ash Road at anything before, and the expressions on their faces didn't suggest they were here to enjoy themselves.

And if this really was meant to be fun, I didn't know why Zana had invited Mr Pifflebackalack.

The school hall was set up with rows of chairs. The Ash Road pupils sat on one side, the Oak Lane ones on the other. The stage was decorated with a set of heavy red curtains, and right in front of the stage was the judges' table, where the two headteachers sat. Mr Pifflebackalack had brought his own "Head Judge" badge.

All of us who had volunteered to compete were gathered at the side of the stage, hidden by the curtains – Oak Lane on one side, Ash Road on the other. I didn't have any talents, but Zana said I could stay with her for something called moral support. Saira was doing some elaborate stretches to get ready for her karate performance. Lucy was organizing her set of paints. Arnold was holding a set of what he said were juggling clubs. I didn't know what juggling was, but Arnold told me it was easy and it didn't matter that he hadn't done it before.

"Where are the gorillas?" I asked Zana, peering out into the hall. "I thought this was all for them."

"They're not actually coming to watch," Zana replied. "We raise money and then we send it to them. Or, I guess, to the people looking after them. A gorilla wouldn't know what to do with money!"

She laughed. I didn't. This talent show was going to be more boring than I'd thought.

Mr Pifflebackalack stood up and clapped his hands once. The half of the hall filled with Ash Road pupils went totally silent. Ms Ashworth quickly stood up and clapped her hands. The Oak Lane half of the hall slowly dribbled down into a quiet murmur.

“Welcome!” Mr Pifflebackalack announced.

“Er, shouldn’t I be saying that?” Ms Ashworth muttered to him. “This is *my* school.”

Mr Pifflebackalack ignored her. "I hereby declare the opening of the inaugural Contest to Determine the Most Elite Talents."

"Catchy name," said Lucy.

"This competition will decide once and for all which of our schools is best. I have selected the crème de la crème of Ash Road to compete, and I have designed a complex judging algorithm to award points to the most deserving pupils," Mr Pifflebackalack continued.

"Have you?" Ms Ashworth spluttered. "I thought this was more of a fun, collaborative thing—"

"There is no point in doing this if nobody wins," Mr Pifflebackalack snapped. "Let us begin!"

Arnold waved his juggling clubs in the air to get the attention of all the Oak Lane competitors waiting to go on stage.

"Listen up, everyone!" he called. "You heard what he said: this is our chance to beat those stinky Ash Road losers once and for all. We all need to get on that stage and totally destroy them!"

"No, no!" Zana cried. "It's not about destroying anyone. It's about having fun and making friends!"

But no one was listening to Zana.

"First on stage," we heard Ms Ashworth announce, "for a 'paint-off' – is that a thing? Never mind. Please would Lucy and Elliott take to the stage."

Lucy and Elliott strode out from behind the curtains at opposite sides of the stage, each carrying something called an easel. They nodded at each other, set down their easels, turned their backs on the audience, and started to paint.

The room was quiet. Someone at the back coughed.

Ms Ashworth shuffled in her seat. "How long is this going to take? It's not very entertaining to watch."

Mr Pifflebackalack peered at the easels. Both of them were painting a bouquet of flowers, but all they'd managed so far was a few green strokes.

"I think we've seen enough to judge," he said. "I declare Ash Road the winners of Round One!"

"What?" Ms Ashworth spluttered. "Hang on, they've barely painted anything, how can you—"

Mr Pifflebackalack glared at her. "Do YOU have a sophisticated judging algorithm?"

Ms Ashworth shrank back. "Well ... er ... no ... I'm just looking at what they've done and..."

"Exactly." Mr Pifflebackalack clapped his hands together once. "NEXT!"

The Oak Lane half of the audience were starting to grumble. Lucy and Elliott shrugged and wandered off stage.

"Next is the keepy-uppy competition: please would Jaden from Oak Lane and

Daniel from Ash Road take to the stage."

As the talent show went on, the challenges changed but the result remained the same. Daniel miskicked the ball, but even as it bounced off stage, Ash Road was declared the winner. No matter how well the Oak Lane pupils performed, Mr Pifflebackalack awarded the win to Ash Road, and Ms Ashworth was powerless to stop him. In the spelling contest, the yo-yo showdown and the knit-off, no matter what happened, Ash Road won. Their half of the audience sat in silence, while our side was getting increasingly annoyed, booing and jeering.

"This is ridiculous!" exclaimed Saira. "They're cheating!"

"You're up next," Zana told her. "Remember, it doesn't matter who Mr Pifflebackalack says is the winner – the point is to have fun."

"Whatever," said Saira, marching over to the stage. "There's no way *I'm* going to lose!"

Saira and Heather took up their positions in the middle of the stage, and started their karate routine. Ms Ashworth had banned them from

actually fighting, so they were performing a sequence of kicks, punches and steps side by side, both scowling intensely with concentration. It was hard to tell who was doing it better; they seemed perfectly in sync. Even so, I could see Mr Pifflebackalack rising to his feet, ready to declare the winner.

Saira spotted this too. And she was not about to be called a loser.

"Ladies and gentlemen," she announced. "Get ready to see the most advanced move in martial arts: the *meia lua de compasso*!"

"Uh oh," Zana muttered to me. "She definitely

hasn't learnt that in her karate class..."

"You might want to move out of the way," Saira warned Heather.

"Never!" Heather replied. "There's no way you can do the *meia lua de compasso*! That's not even karate!"

"Can so! Just watch!"

Saira bent forward. She put her hands on the ground. She started to spin. She lifted her leg ... and kicked Heather right in the bum.

It wasn't a very powerful kick – Saira was falling backwards, flailing, as she did it – but it was enough to send Heather toppling over.

Mr Pifflebackalack leapt out of his chair. "I knew I would regret approving this tomfoolery! Your pupils are out of control!"

Ms Ashworth jumped up too. "She just made a mistake. She didn't mean to—"

"I do not want to hear it! My pupil has been attacked. We could all be in danger!" Mr Pifflebackalack turned to his side of the audience. "Ash Road, back to class!"

As the Ash Road pupils trooped out of the hall, I patted Zana on the back. "At least no one threw any milkshakes."

20

The good news was that Ms Ashworth was so annoyed with Mr Pifflebackalack that she forgot to tell Saira off for ruining the talent show. The bad news was ... pretty much everything else. Not only had the show failed to bring the schools happily together and end the fighting, it had caused more embarrassment for Oak Lane. And it had also made Saira and Arnold more annoyed at each other.

"I never even got the chance to do my juggling routine," Arnold muttered that afternoon. We were working in groups to make maps in geography class, while Mr Martins had a cup of tea and watched *Antiques Roadshow* on his laptop. "It was going to be the most amazing thing anyone had ever seen. It would have won the whole talent show. And you ruined it by being rubbish at martial arts."

Saira threw down the blue crayon she was using to colour in the sea. "If you're so great at juggling, Arnold, you're welcome to show us any time."

Arnold went red. "No. I'm too upset now. I'll never juggle again."

"You've never juggled before," Lucy pointed out.

All this fighting was making my head hurt. I couldn't wait for the bell to ring for the end of the day. Sadly, when it did ring, it brought something even worse: Ms Ashworth. With the caretaker on strike ever since the milkshake incident, she was looking for someone to clear up the chairs in the hall, and that someone was going to be Zana. Which meant it was also going to be me.

So while the rest of the school made a dash for the school gates, Zana and I traipsed back to the hall. Arnold refused to help us, but he did agree to wait outside for me because I couldn't be trusted to find my way to his house on my own.

We started slowly dragging and stacking the rows of chairs.

“Fixing the planet isn’t going very well, is it?” said Zana.

“Even worse than my last visit,” I agreed.

“I’m sorry that all my plans have ended in disaster,” Zana sighed.

“It wasn’t your fault that we threw milkshakes, or that Mr Pifflebackalack was cheating, or that Saira thought she could do the most advanced move in martial arts without any practice.”

“No, but I should have realized that those ideas were the wrong way to stop the fighting.” Zana paused and leant against a stack of chairs. “I have one final idea. Really, it’s what we should have done right at the beginning. But I have to warn you: it’s very sensible and boring and it might be difficult.”

Those were a few of my least favourite things. But if it helped fix my problem, I didn’t have much choice. I sighed. “What is it?”

“Peace talks,” said Zana. “We all sit down together, we discuss our issues, we stop blaming each other and we apologize. No chance for misunderstandings, or sabotage, or martial arts. Just talking.”

I slumped down on one of the chairs. "Urgh. Boring."

"I know," admitted Zana. "But I do think it will work. I've been watching lots of YouTube videos on how to successfully negotiate. Apparently we have to listen actively and put ourselves in their shoes."

"What if they don't fit?"

"It's a metaphor," said Zana. "As in, we've got to see things from their point of view if we're going to build bridges."

"Arnold and I tried building a drawbridge already. It's harder than it looks."

"Maybe I'd better stop using metaphors," said Zana. "The point is, this fighting is getting worse and worse, and we need to stop it before someone gets hurt."

"Someone already got hurt. I got kicked in the bum."

"ARGH!" Zana and I both jumped. We hadn't noticed Heather standing in the door of the hall.

"Heather," Zana said in a wobbly voice. "What are you doing here? Is it your karate class?"

"It's not two o'clock in the morning already, is it?" I checked.

"No," said Heather. She looked at Zana. "I came here looking for you."

"Oh, to keep bullying her?" I asked.

"No," said Heather, frowning. "Did you think I was bullying you?"

Zana stood up as tall as she could. "I didn't *think* you were bullying me. You *were* bullying me."

"I guess I have been a bit mean," Heather admitted. "Sorry about that. I got caught up in this whole school rivalry thing. That's why I wanted to come and find you. I actually wanted to say thanks."

"I think this is a trap," I whispered to Zana. Arnold had made me very suspicious about this kind of thing.

"Shh, Sky," said Zana. "What did you want to say thanks for?"

"For giving me the opportunity to show off how great I am," Heather replied. "I mean, I knew I would beat Saira easily in our karate-off, but I never thought she'd make me look SO brilliant. It was totally worth a kick in the bum."

"I'm glad you enjoyed it," Zana said. "It just goes to show that good things can happen when you work together, instead of fighting."

Heather shrugged. "Maybe. I would say it goes to show that I'm the best at karate, but your thing makes sense too, I guess."

"Well, seeing as you enjoyed it so much, maybe you can help with clearing up the chairs?" I suggested. One of my special skills was spotting opportunities for me to do less work. Heather rolled her eyes, but agreed.

We stacked the chairs in silence for a few minutes. I saw Elliott and Lucy wander past the window, carrying between them a massive orange pot, decorated with swirly patterns. All of a sudden, Arnold burst through the hall doors.

"Look out!" he yelled. "Heather from Ash Road has infiltrated the school!"

"We know," said Zana. "She's right there."

Heather waved.

"How did it take you so long to notice?" I asked.

Arnold rubbed the back of his neck. "Er ... I was round the corner. Practising my juggling. On an unrelated note, do you have a ladder? Somehow my juggling clubs have ended up on the roof."

"You know Elliott's here as well?" I told Arnold.

"What?! This is a total invasion!" Arnold cried, and dashed back out to keep watch for any more surprise guests from Ash Road.

I noticed that Zana was squinting at Heather strangely. I recognized that face. It was the face of someone thinking very hard to come up with a plan. When Zana smiled, I knew she'd succeeded.

"Say, Heather," she said slowly. "What would you think about working together on something?"

"Working together?" I whispered to Zana, as Heather considered her offer. "Don't you need to get revenge for her bullying you?"

Zana shook her head. "If I get revenge, then she

gets revenge, and then I get revenge back… It'll never stop."

"So you're just going to be friends now, easy as that?"

"I never said we were going to be friends," Zana corrected me. "But we don't need to be. We just need to stop fighting."

Heather was watching us whispering with her arms folded. "Is this another prank?" she asked.

"Not this time," Zana promised her. "We need your help. We're going to organize peace talks between Oak Lane and Ash Road – this Friday, after school. Bring the Enviro Club. We're going to stop this fight once and for all."

21

Tidying the school hall took for ever, but eventually we were allowed to go home. It was actually better taking the bus a bit later; there weren't so many Ash Road pupils around to point and laugh at us.

"We need some fresh ideas," said Arnold, as we approached his front door. "Maybe you should transfer to their school? You could go undercover, plant whoopee cushions in the staff room, that kind of thing."

Arnold unlocked the front door and opened it.

"Actually," I said, "Zana has a plan for—"

WHUMP!

A pillow flew through the front door and hit Arnold in the face. He staggered backwards.

I frowned. That had never happened before.

BOUFFFFF!

A cushion spun through the air and bounced off the top of my head.

I looked at Arnold. "OK, now we know that definitely wasn't an accident."

"Take cover – they're attacking us!" Arnold yelled. He grabbed my arm and dragged me inside, into the sitting room and behind the sofa.

"What's going on?" I asked, as another pillow zipped over our heads and struck the wall behind us.

"Pillow fight!" Arnold replied.

I grabbed the nearby pillow and punched it.

"You don't fight the pillows, you fight WITH them," Arnold explained. "Try to hit one of my brothers!"

Arnold grabbed the pillow off me and launched it over the sofa. "Take that!" he yelled. It hit nobody. Arnold ducked back down just as a cushion came back the other way.

“It’s no good,” Arnold said.

“Your throwing?” I asked.

“No! The situation. We’re outnumbered. Also, we haven’t got any pillows. We’re going to have to make a run for it.” Arnold grabbed me by the shoulders. “If either one of us doesn’t make it, it’s been nice knowing you.”

This worried me. Normally Arnold would have said it was pretty annoying knowing me. He must be really panicking.

Arnold leapt out from behind the sofa and sprinted for the stairs. I followed, feeling my human heart dancing about in my chest. Out of the corner of my eye, I saw Brother 1 looming out of the kitchen doorway, holding a long blue pillow over his head.

“THE TRAVEL PILLOW!” Arnold squealed in horror. “Every man for themselves!”

Arnold launched himself up the stairs. I wasn’t quick enough. The blue horror spun through the air towards me...

BOING!

It bounced off my head, and I remembered that pillows were actually quite soft. Arnold must have forgotten that, as he was scrambling away, shrieking.

I ran upstairs after him and followed him into his bedroom.

“Shut the door!” he shouted. I did, just as a cushion hit the other side with a dull thud.

“I thought I was a goner,” Arnold breathed. “Sorry about leaving you behind. I did say every man for himself.”

“It’s fine, it didn’t hurt,” I said. I slumped down next to Arnold on the edge of his bed. “Seems like your brothers are still pretty mad at you.”

Arnold sighed. “Yeah. I thought this fight with Ash Road would make them like me, but now we’re losing, they think I’m embarrassing them.” He rubbed his face where one of the cushions had hit. “I thought you were going to stop them ganging up on me?”

Maybe it was my chat with Zana. Maybe one of the pillows had hit me hard enough to jog my brain into gear. Whatever it was, I was experiencing an unusual sensation: I had an idea.

"You need to make peace with your brothers," I said. "You need to hold peace talks."

OK, so maybe it wasn't really my idea. I was just repeating what Zana had said to me earlier. But that didn't mean it wasn't good.

"It's not like you to have a good idea." Arnold tilted his head to one side, thinking. "I wouldn't usually agree, but I'm willing to try anything at this point. Plus, I don't want to get a pillow in my face when I'm eating my dinner." He nodded – that decided it. "Let's do it."

That evening, we sat down for our peace talks.

Well, we sat down for dinner. Arnold said there was no way his brothers would show up if he invited them for peace talks, so we'd have to catch them unawares. So I donned my latest disguise of sunglasses and a witch's hat, and we prepared to do battle. Peacefully.

"Why did you let Ash Road humiliate us at the talent show?" Brother 1 demanded, once he'd finished shovelling his food into his mouth.

I slowly got up out of my chair.

“Yeah, you made us all look like losers,” Brother 2 agreed.

I edged round the table to find a clear space on the floor.

“I’m sorry you feel that way,” Arnold said. He had watched some YouTube videos about how to do a peace talk before dinner. “And I want you to know that I hear what you’re saying.”

“Of course you can hear what they’re saying,” said Brother 3. “They’re sitting right next to you.”

I took a deep breath and reached out my arms.

"I want you to treat this as a safe space to share your frustrations," Arnold continued. "Tell me what you think the..." He trailed off. "Sorry, Sky, what *are* you doing?"

I paused my star jumps. "Active listening."

"Sit down!"

"What's going on here?" Brother 4 demanded. "Your friend is acting weird and you're talking weird."

Arnold took a deep breath. "We're just trying to... I want to... You guys... I'm sick of you all ganging up on me and throwing pillows at me and messing with my action figures, and it's not fair!" he squeaked.

There was a long silence. Arnold's dad poked his head round the door.

"Everything OK in here?" he asked wearily.

We all nodded. Arnold's dad blinked at me.

"My friend Fry," Arnold explained. His dad shrugged and disappeared.

"Arnold," said Brother 4. "We didn't realize you were so upset."

Brother 3 patted him on the arm. "We were just trying to have a bit of fun."

Arnold sniffed. “It’s not felt very fun. Especially all the pressure you put on me to win the fight with Ash Road.”

“Well, we’re sorry,” said Brother 2.

I couldn’t believe what I was seeing through my sunglasses. The peace talk plan was actually working! Was this the easy solution I’d been looking for all along?

“I’ve got an idea,” Brother 1 piped up. “Why don’t we work together to beat Ash Road?”

“Yeah!” agreed Brother 3. “I don’t know why you’re messing about with talent shows. What you need is a proper showdown.”

Arnold sat up in his seat. “Like the Awesome Squad have! There’s always a big fight with the baddies, at the end of every episode.”

“Right,” agreed Brother 2. “And I know exactly how you do it.”

“How?”

Brothers 1, 2, 3 and 4 grinned. “Pillow fight!”

Arnold punched the air. “Yeah!”

Brother 4 whipped out his mobile phone. “I’ll get the word out to everyone at Ash Road. Friday. After school. You guys tell everyone in your classes at Oak Lane. This is going to be mega."

I felt a bit light-headed, and not from the star jumps. Friday afternoon was when Zana was organizing her peace talks. I would have told Arnold this, except he wouldn't have heard me, because he was chanting "PILLOW FIGHT! PILLOW FIGHT!" with his brothers.

And I would have told him after that, except then we actually did have another pillow fight, as practice for Friday, and it's hard to talk when cushions keep bopping you in the face.

And I would have told him later, before he went to sleep, except ... well, to be honest, by then I had forgotten about it all.

22

In my defence, I didn't see any reason why Zana's peace talks couldn't go ahead. After all, now I had seen them work, I did believe that she could use them to stop the fight between the two schools. But Arnold was also talking very convincingly about how the pillow fight showdown would be the final boss battle between the schools, the fight to end all fights, and that sounded like a good way to solve my problem too.

That was when I had my next brilliant idea: I would let Zana and Arnold both try out their plans. On Friday afternoon, Zana could hold her peace talks, and Arnold could launch his pillow fight. One of them HAD to work.

Sometimes I wondered if my time on Earth was turning me into a genius.

The only problem was, I had to make sure that neither of them found out about the other's plan. For a while, I managed to keep them away from each other by telling both of them that the other one hadn't brushed their teeth that morning and had awful smelly breath. (I knew a lot about this because I'd been on Earth for a long time before anyone told me I needed to brush my teeth.)

But that trick couldn't work for ever. On Friday morning, we were in maths class, making three-dimensional shapes out of building blocks while Mr Martins sat with his feet on his desk. I was finding this very challenging. Where I'm from, we have over 400 dimensions.

Zana leant across to me. "I keep hearing people talking about a pillow fight with Ash Road."

"I keep hearing them too," I replied. It was easier not to lie.

"I hope that wasn't your idea," said Zana.

"No, it wasn't," I said. Which was also true. It was Arnold's.

“It’s probably just a wild rumour,” said Zana. “Besides, once our peace talks are finished this afternoon, nobody will want to fight.” She squinted at something under the desk next to us. “Does Arnold have a bag of pillows?”

I knew the answer to this was yes, as that morning Arnold and I had raided all the beds and cupboards in his house for every pillow and cushion his brothers hadn’t already seized. I didn’t want to tell Zana this, though. So I threw my 3D model in the air, and watched as it crashed down onto the floor, sending little bricks skidding everywhere and making Mr Martins sit up with a jolt.

"Sky!" cried Zana.

"Sorry, I was trying to add the eighth dimension to my model."

By lunchtime, I was really struggling to keep the two plans secret. Eco Club sat down together, and in desperation I asked Zana to tell us more about the gorilla sanctuary. No one else had a chance to talk about anything once Zana got going. But soon, disaster struck.

"OK, I think we've heard enough about the grooming habits of gorillas," sighed Arnold. "Now, is everyone ready for this afternoon's p—"

"PICNIC!" I blurted out.

Arnold frowned at me. "No… I was talking about the p—"

"POTATO!" I cut in.

"Sky, it's very rude to keep interrupting," said Zana. "I'm glad to hear Arnold is looking forward to the p—"

"PIFFLEBACKALACK!" I shouted, pointing out of the window.

"I don't see him," said Lucy. Neither did I, because he wasn't actually there.

"He must have run off," I said.

"Come on guys, we'd better find out what he's up to!" Saira ordered.

We charged out of the canteen to search for the headteacher. I was grateful that both "pillow fight" and "peace talks" started with the same letter, or there was no way I'd have got away with that.

As the bell rang for the end of the day, I dodged Arnold and hurried after Zana as she made her way to the school hall.

"Heather should be here with Enviro Crew any minute," Zana said, looking across at the school gates. "Oh, is that her now? She's brought an awful lot of people..."

Zana was right. There was a huge group of Ash Road pupils massing at the school gates, swinging pillows above their heads as menacingly as they could. Which wasn't very – it's hard to make a pillow look menacing.

Arnold bounded up behind us, clapping a pair of cushions together. "Here we go, guys! Winner takes all! The fight of the century!"

Zana turned to face me. She had the same look on her face as she had in art class when I poured paint all over her picture to try to get it finished quicker. I knew this meant she was disappointed.

"Did you know about this, Sky?" she asked.

"Er ... yes."

"Why didn't you tell me?" Zana cried. "I thought you supported my peace talks plan?"

"I did," I said, honestly.

Heather strode up to us. She had pillows tied round her waist and up her arms. I didn't know if you could be a professional pillow fighter, but she certainly looked like one.

"Thought you could trick me, did you?" she said to Zana. "And to think I trusted you! Do you know how silly you made me look, going round Ash Road inviting everyone to peace talks, telling them Oak Lane was ready to apologize? Then I find out you were planning on ambushing us with pillows as soon as we arrived!"

"No, it's not like that – I didn't know this was planned!" Zana insisted.

"Whatever." Heather pulled one of the pillows

off her belt and prodded Zana with it. "When the fight starts, I'll have my revenge!"

Heather charged off to join the Ash Road ranks at the other side of the playground. Beside us, Oak Lane pupils were gathering. I could see Brother 1 with his trusty travel pillow.

"What have you done, Sky?" Zana whispered. "I thought I'd shown you that fighting isn't the answer. You're never going to fix your planet this way."

"I just thought we could try both plans at the same time," I tried to explain. "Come on, start your peace talks!"

Zana shook her head. "It's too late for that now. I've tried to help you, Sky. I've done everything I can."

And with that, Zana walked off. Which meant I had no choice: it was Arnold's plan or failure.

I didn't like either of those options.

23

A bird circled ominously over the school playground. A breeze fluttered the flags someone had made out of blankets. Loose pillow feathers drifted across the no-man's land between the two groups of Oak Lane and Ash Road pupils. Everyone was poised for battle.

(The atmosphere was slightly ruined by the bird, which pooed on Saira's shoulder.)

I found Arnold standing a couple of rows back on the Oak Lane side, right behind Rude Jaden, who was bouncing up and down with excitement. Lucy was next to him, although she hadn't brought any pillows and was looking round at everyone like they'd lost their minds. I couldn't see Zana. I guessed she'd gone home, so she didn't have to witness the fight. A little churning, like I usually got after I'd eaten a more unusual piece of human food, started up in my stomach. Zana had told me before that this feeling didn't always mean I needed to run to the nearest toilet. Sometimes it meant I was feeling guilty; like it was my body telling me I might not be doing the right thing. That maybe Zana was right, and that maybe I was wrong to betray my friend.

But I wasn't on Earth to make friends. I was here to stop a fight.

"I'm going straight for Alma," Arnold muttered, nodding in her direction. I could see her whirling her cushions above her head, her face scrunched in fury.

"Are you still playing chess online with her?"

Arnold's grip on his cushion slipped. "What? I mean … yes. I am. What's that got to do with anything?"

"I don't know," I said, rubbing my stomach and hoping the unsettling feeling would go away. "It sounds like the kind of thing friends do. But you're about to try to hit her with a cushion."

Arnold scowled. "Because we've got to win this fight, Sky! Stop making me think about things."

I wished I could stop thinking about things, because I hated doing that. And it was too late to change course now anyway. Across the playground, the Ash Road pupils were preparing to charge. The Oak Lane pupils behind us waited for a signal. Saira, who was leading from the front as usual, raised her pillow in the air...

And then I saw it. Something that made me feel like I'd been hit in the stomach with a pillow stuffed with carrots (which I was sure would be against the rules). Something so unexpected, I had to rub my eyes, which actually made them blurrier, so then I had to blink several times until I could see clearly again. And then there was no doubting it: there was a shock of blue hair making its way through the crowd of Ash Road pupils.

Zana stepped out, clutching a pillow.

"Zana, you're on the wrong side!" I called. "Oak Lane are over here!"

Zana called back, "I've switched allegiances."

"What does that mean?"

"Sides! I've switched sides."

A gasp went up. Although only from Eco Club, as the rest of the school didn't really care about what Zana was doing.

"What do you mean?" I called.

"She's explained it pretty clearly," Arnold snapped, from beside me. "She's a traitor! Let's aim for her first."

"Wait!" I told him. "Zana, why are you doing this?"

"Because it's the only way to make you think about what you're doing," Zana shouted. "If you really think fighting is the answer. If you really don't care about who gets hurt. Prove it. Fight me."

I lifted my pillow.

But the pillow suddenly felt heavier. And it wasn't because I'd put carrots in it. I looked across at Zana. I knew what she liked, what made her laugh, what she wanted to do when she grew up. Well, she'd told me these things – I wasn't sure I remembered them all. But I remembered how Zana made me feel. How she looked after me, and stopped me being expelled or taken away by the authorities for questioning.

And I knew I couldn't fight her.

I pushed my way through the Oak Lane army and walked across the playground, towards the massed Ash Road pupils. Zana walked forward to meet me.

"Let's end the fighting," Zana said to me. "Together."

I nodded.

We tossed our pillows aside with as much force as we could manage.

Unfortunately, this was the exact moment that Mr Pifflebackalack arrived.

"What in the name of— *OOOOF*!"

Our pillows hit him right in the face. He stumbled backwards, lost his footing and tumbled, rolling down the slope away from the playground.

This was quite unfortunate. What was even more unfortunate was what Mr Pifflebackalack was rolling towards.

Because our caretaker had gone on strike, no one had cleared up the supply of milkshakes that Arnold and I had stored behind the school hall. I don't know if you've ever smelled milkshake that's been left in the sun for more than a week, but if you have, your nose has probably fallen off.

And this was what Mr Pifflebackalack landed SPLAT in the middle of.

"NONSENSE!" Mr Pifflebackalack squealed. He tried to stand up, but the milkshake was too slippery. He slid around on his hands

and knees, trapped. “SILLINESS! INANITY! GOBBLEDEGOOK!”

“Oops,” I said.

Arnold ran over to me and Zana. “What did you do that for? We’re really in for it now!”

“What do you mean?” I asked, having to shout to be heard over Mr Pifflebackalack’s yelping.

“You took out Ash Road’s leader!” Arnold cried. “They’re going to be determined to get revenge! They’re not going to take any prisoners! They’re... Oh. They’re laughing?”

Arnold was right. (For once.) The Oak Lane pupils were laughing, of course – we all hated Mr Pifflebackalack. But the Ash Road pupils on the other side of the playground were also laughing at their headteacher. They were giggling. They were snorting. Someone was actually hooting.

“Oh,” I said. “Does this mean the pillow fight is cancelled?”

24

The playground was filled with the sound of laughter. And, faintly, the squelching of milkshake.

Daniel was at the front of the Ash Road army, wiping tears from his eyes.

"What's going on?" Arnold demanded. "Why aren't you wreaking vengeance on us for eliminating your beloved leader?"

"Beloved leader?" Daniel repeated. "Who, Mr Pifflebackalack?!"

This made him laugh even more, and we had to wait until he'd caught his breath and could speak again.

"Everyone at Ash Road *hates* Mr Pifflebackalack!" Daniel told us.

"You do?" said Zana. "But, ever since he joined

your school, you've won everything! There's not a single sport we can beat you at."

"That's true," Daniel replied. Then he shrugged. "But winning feels pretty rubbish when you don't enjoy it. He makes us train all the time. And no one can even quit the sports' teams, because then he gives you extra homework."

The rest of the Enviro Crew and Eco Club emerged out of the crowds of pupils. Heather was peeling off the pillows she'd strapped to herself. Elliott dropped the cushion he hadn't looked that interested in holding. Even Alma's face was relaxing out of its usual grimace.

"What's going on?" demanded Saira. "Why's no one hitting each other?"

"I think it's pretty hard to laugh and hit someone at the same time," Lucy pointed out.

"That was funny, what you did to Mr Pifflebackalack," Heather said. "If there's anyone who deserves to get hit with a pillow, it's him."

"Yeah, he's a nightmare," Alma agreed. "He even managed to suck the fun out of chess. And you'd think that was impossible." She raised an eyebrow at Arnold. "Maybe instead of messing about with duels and pillow fights, we should set up a proper chess tournament."

Arnold hadn't quite relaxed his grip on his pillows, but he gave a small nod. "I guess that could be cool. It would be nice to have someone else to hang out with."

Arnold glanced at me. I wasn't sure why. I did a special one-eyed blink at him. He looked confused. It seemed like I still hadn't got the hang of that one.

"That's a great idea," Zana jumped in. "Because if there's one thing I learnt from the talent competition – apart from the fact that Saira can't do the *meia lua de compasso* – it's that we actually all have loads in common. Like, Lucy and Elliott, you both like art!"

Lucy and Elliott gave Zana a matching look – as though she'd just told them that grass was green.

"We've literally been working on a pottery project together all term," said Lucy.

"Yeah, it was pretty obvious we liked the same things," added Elliott.

“Well that’s silly, because you were supposed to be fighting.” Saira sniffed. “And I can too do the *meia lua de compasso*. The stage was slippery, that’s all – it threw me off balance.”

“Whatever,” said Heather. “Although, if you wanted to learn some more martial arts, maybe we could take a class together?”

“Maybe,” said Saira with a shrug. “As long as you don’t mind me being better at it than you. And as long as Zana fixes her app so we don’t have to do it at two in the morning.”

As Eco Club and Enviro Crew kept chatting, without once whoomphing each other in the face with a pillow, I whispered to Zana, “Seems like you were right about the peace talks.”

Zana grinned at me. “Sky, I think we just ended the fight.”

"Kind of accidentally," I pointed out.

"It doesn't matter," Zana said. "Everyone is realizing that it's better not to fight."

"It's better to laugh at your teachers."

"Yes. That's exactly the message to take away here."

We watched the Ash Road and Oak Lane pupils mingling on the playground, filming Mr Pifflebackalack on their phones as he continued to flail in the pile of milkshake.

Zana said, "You know, this has all solved itself pretty neatly, hasn't it?"

"WHAT ON EARTH IS GOING ON?!"

A silence descended over the playground. Ms Ashworth had burst out of her office, and stood with her hands on her hips and her eyebrows pointing sharply down, like they were trying to escape to her chin.

Zana gulped. "Ah. Maybe not so neatly, after all."

Arnold hid behind me. "I can't get suspended again! It was so boring!"

Ms Ashworth surveyed the scene: the dozens of Ash Road pupils, the drifting feathers and abandoned pillows, and, finally, Mr Pifflebackalack, slithering and slipping in the milkshake. I checked my pocket to see if my trans-dimensional transporter was there. It looked like I was going to need a quick exit to avoid the terrible punishment Ms Ashworth was about to unleash.

The Head raised a single, trembling finger. She directed it at Mr Pifflebackalack. And she let out an almighty, ground-shaking, "HAHA!"

She quickly covered her mouth and looked round, as if she was checking if anyone had heard her. Which we all had, because, as I mentioned, it was ground-shakingly loud.

Ms Ashworth strode quickly over to us. "Children, I want to be clear that it is never kind to laugh at someone else's misfortune. Even when it is quite

funny. Now, is anyone going to tell me what's going on here?"

Arnold peered over my shoulder. "It wasn't our fault, Miss! It was total coincidence that everyone turned up at the same time with pillows, and Mr Pifflebackalack just fell over, I swear. Please don't suspend us!"

"Suspend you? Now, why would I do that?" Ms Ashworth glanced over her shoulder at Mr Pifflebackalack. "I can't stand that man. Perhaps now he's had a bath in rotten milkshake, he might stop thinking he's so much better than me. Now come on, clear off, it's Friday and we've all got better places to be."

I wondered if the place she had to be was riding a donkey. Or maybe that was only Saturday mornings.

Ms Ashworth hesitated before she walked off. "Did someone get a photo of Mr Piffleback-a-chops, by the way?"

Saira nodded. "Loads. And videos."

Ms Ashworth gave us a small smile. "Excellent."

25

I had set out to stop one fight, and I had done it – just in time. I was surer than I'd ever been that I would return home and get the grade I needed to move on from this terrible project.

I didn't, however, go home straight away. Because although we had avoided punishment from Ms Ashworth, the area outside the school hall was now smeared with milkshake and, even worse, pillows and feathers soaked in milkshake, and the caretaker was refusing to come back to work until it was cleaned up. And I could have left Arnold to do it on his own. But Zana had asked me not to. And she said if I stayed, she'd help us clear it up. So, I did.

I was getting good at this friends thing.

On Saturday morning, we pulled on rubber boots and rubber gloves and set to work. Zana's parents had let me have a sleepover at their house the night before, mainly because she had promised that it was the last time they would see me. As a special treat, we watched a movie about my old friends, the dinosaurs. Once I'd got over my disappointment that these dinosaurs weren't real and we couldn't actually visit this Jurassic Park, I enjoyed it. Especially the bits where the dinosaurs ate the humans.

Arnold arrived late, and grumpy.

"Cheer up," said Zana. "If we all work together, we can have this finished in no time."

"It's not that." Arnold picked up a sodden pillow and winced. "Well, it's partly that. But I'm also annoyed because my brothers put hairbrushes inside my shoes this morning. I thought I'd trodden on a hedgehog."

I dropped the cushion I was holding. "I thought I solved the fight with your brothers? We had peace talks and everything!"

"That's just brothers being brothers, Sky," Zana said. "Some things never change."

"Well, at least I solved your bully problem," I said.

"Did you? I mean, you were there when it happened, but I don't know that you actually did anything to..." Zana trailed off as she saw me glaring at her with my hands on my hips. My grade was never going to improve if no one would give me credit for fixing any of their problems. "Of course, you did help me. Thank you."

"You're welcome." I tried to wipe off the milkshake that I had just smeared onto myself. Putting my hands on my hips had not been a good move.

"In fact, Heather is actually helping me organize a joint outing for Eco Club and Enviro Crew," Zana continued.

"Oh cool!" Arnold piped up. "What are we doing? Bowling? Laser tag? Go-karting?"

Zana avoided his gaze as she brushed up some feathers on the ground. "We're doing a litter pick by the river."

I didn't think it was possible, but Arnold looked even more annoyed.

"Heather is still being quite difficult," admitted Zana. "But that doesn't matter, because I'm the bigger person."

I was pretty sure Heather was taller than Zana, but maybe she was planning on growing.

We were interrupted by Ms Ashworth marching across the playground. She was wearing a harness that trailed huge multi-coloured fabric behind her.

"I've got good news!" she announced.

"Is it that we can stop cleaning up this rotten milkshake?" Arnold guessed.

"No. Mr Pifflebackalack has gone viral!"

Ms Ashworth showed us her phone. She scrolled

through dozens of clips of Mr Pifflebackalack, sliding around in the pile of milkshake. Each one had captions like: "LOL epic teacher fail" and "My milkshake brings all the headteachers to the yard".

"All over the internet!" Ms Ashworth exclaimed. "Mr Pifflebackalack has quit his job and is moving to Liechtenstein."

"Why Liechtenstein?" asked Zana.

"He said it's the most nonsense-free place on Earth." She stuffed her phone back in her pocket. "Anyway, I must dash. I'm on my way to my indoor parachuting class. I just wanted to let you know that, despite your *many* faults, you've actually made a positive difference. I will no longer be bothered by that little grey man!"

Zana smiled at me. "How about that, Sky? Making a positive difference to the planet."

"I wouldn't go that far," said Arnold.

I ignored him. There was a warm feeling in my tummy. I grinned back at Zana. "At this rate, I might even be top of the class!"

Arnold stared at us. "What are you guys on about?"

Although we'd promised Zana's parents they'd never have to see me again, on Saturday afternoon, once we'd finished our cleaning, we snuck back to Zana's room. Zana said it wasn't often she got the chance to see someone zap themselves into another dimension (in fact, it had only happened once before).

"It was good to see you again, Sky," said Zana. "I know Earth is not your favourite place to visit, but it's been nice having you here. Mostly."

"It's not been too bad," I admitted. "Though I'll be glad to finally get home and start learning how to surf black holes."

Zana's mouth dropped open. "You surf black holes?"

"It's not *that* amazing. It's not like it's a worm hole."

"Right..." Zana shook her head. "Will you come and visit again?"

I scratched my chin like Arnold did when he was thinking, or when his brothers had put itching powder on his school tie. "Maybe. It wouldn't be the worst thing in the universe."

"Really?"

"No. That would be having to sit through another cricket match." I got the slime that disguised my trans-dimensional transporter out of my pocket. "I'll keep an eye out for your lizard."

"Er... Why would Berners-Lee be in another dimension?"

"Don't know. Doesn't matter. The important thing is – thank you, Zana. For all your help. As humans go, you're really not bad."

Zana broke into such a massive grin that it seemed like it might stretch her face permanently.

"Goodbye, Sky. And don't worry. I am pretty confident that *this* time you've done enough to get a good grade."

I nodded. I activated my transporter. And I went home.

26

I won't lie to you: I didn't exactly get a passing grade. But my teacher had enjoyed the peace and quiet while I was on Earth so much, they let me have a go at black-hole surfing.

I fell off.

Acknowledgements

The problem with writing a second book is that you end up promising a lot of people who you didn't acknowledge in the first book that you'd acknowledge them in this book instead. The following people I'm either very grateful to, or have guilt-tripped me. I'll let you decide which is which.

My thanks and eternal gratitude go to Becky Watson, Laurissa Jones, Clo Tartinville, Frances Taffinder, Sarah Handley and Jack Noel.

For helping me come up with character names and generally being brilliant, thank you to my lovely friends Lauren Edwards, Melissa Hunt, Alex Lacey, Jemma Marshall, Sandie McKenzie, Helena Miles, Sophie Morgan, Charlotte Morris, Ruth Oxlade and Rosie Pain.

I'd also like to thank my long-time partner-in-(writing)-crime Addy Newton. And as I've already name-checked my godmother Auntie Anne in this book, I am obliged to also acknowledge my other godmother Auntie Margaret and emphasize that I don't have a favourite.

Thanks again to everyone at Walker who worked on this book, especially new addition to team TWWA, the wonderful Meera Santiapillai.